He Thought He Had Me

By: Author Jamie

HE THOUGHT HE HAD ME

ISBN: 978-1-945035-04-3

Edited by Black Lyfe Publications

Cover by Kranch Media

Printed in the United States of America

Dedication

I dedicate this to everyone who has ever had a dream and didn't pursue it. I'm here to tell you nothing comes to sleepers but...dreams.

HE THOUGHT HE HAD ME

Dana

"Marques! Do I hear a fucking horn outside? Marques wake the hell up!"

I know damn well this nigga hear me killing this horn. He either coming out or I'm going in.

"Damn Shawna, I'm trying to sleep; fuck that damn horn!"

I wasn't letting up if this bitch gon' keep coming over here. He may as well pack all his shit today.

"Well I think your little girlfriend is going to wake up my damn neighbors, so you need to go check her before I do."

On the scale of 1-10, I know my damn horn blowing was a damn 10 of annoyance. I saw someone peek through the blinds to see who it was, as if he didn't already know it was my ass.

"I'll be right back Shawna, just sit here and don't start no shit!"

I looked back up at the upstairs window and now her bitch ass peeking out the window like that is gonna make me stop. I ain't stopping shit until I see his ass come up out of there.

HE THOUGHT HE HAD ME

I saw the door swing open of course it was Marques he walked up to my damn car like he was a school yard bully.

"What the hell are you doing here Dee?"

"When are you coming home?"

I know as hard minded as I was when I saw him, I lost all composure sniffling and wiping tears through every word I spoke. Marques leaned his head in the car while resting his hands on the door.

"When I get there Dee, so please don't do this shit. I don't feel like doing this shit so fucking early in the damn morning. You bring your ass over here and for what? Cause you all in your feelings and shit. I don't understand why in the world would you come over here and embarrass yourself like this Dee."

"I'm not embarrassing myself! I love you and I want you to come home Marques. Why are you even here with her ass?"

"Like I said, I'll be home when I get there."

I continued to wipe my falling tears. Fuck I wish I had the strength to drive away from him and never return. But love got a hold on me and now I'm a fool in love.

"Oh I see; she can have you whenever she wants, but the one who has put up with all of your shit for three years; you treat like shit!"

"Call it what you want, but if you want me to come home; this isn't the way to go about it."

"So, coming to get my man was wrong?"

My voice cracked with every word I spoke. Marques had no sympathy for my fucking feelings at this point.

He out here talking reckless and this nosey bitch up in the window looking and grinning and shit. This shit has to get better.

"Alright Dee, I'll see you sometime tonight."

This nigga had the nerve to kiss me after saying that shit to me. I watched him turn away from me and walk back to the brick town house where he stayed from time to time.

My heart was in pure distress. I was about to pull off when I noticed Shawna looking at me, smiling and showing a grand thirty-two.

I was in pain as if I had just buried my momma and needed to be reborn again, with no way of seeing the one who has given me life. I hit the Dan Ryan expressway at top speed trying to out run my problems. Going Downtown Chicago to my cozy office was my way to escape the worries of Marques.

I'm a booming photographer for some very wealthy Chicagoans. Whether the pictures are from bouncing bundles of joy or from a couple who wants to pose in the nude, I love what I do. To capture moments that's otherwise missed, is one of the best feeling in the world. And at top dollar, I was going to make sure I kept the camera flashing.

I even snapped pictures of the ones that have tackled marriage and almost lost. The worry lines on their faces gave away history to their relationship. I was really curious to the ones that have made it through the storm. At this point, I'm so unsure of my future with Marques that I'm willing to speak with anyone who had some insight on how to have a better relationship.

I truly understand that my relationship with Marques is not a healthy one, but like most of us women; I put love before brains.

I sat in her high back leather chair and thought about the set of thirty-twos that smiled at me. Thoughts of him and her fucking at this very moment flashed across my mind; fucking me up even more. As much as I wished that they weren't, I knew that was too much like right, for them not to be.

HE THOUGHT HE HAD ME

As I was trying to get my mind off these early mornings events, Michael walked in. He's a great assistant. That's all he'll ever be, even though he has made some gestures letting me know that he is interested. If I wasn't so blindly in love with Marques trifling ass, I would probably give him a shot of this good pussy.

"Hey Dana, we have a nine o'clock in fifteen minutes. I have everything set up for you, so I'll meet you in the photo room."

"Thank you Mike."

Michael stood 6'3 with jet black hair that he kept short and a tight muscular build. Michael worked out four times a week to keep his body in tip top shape. His dark brown eyes was sultry, his chiseled face was adorned by a tapered beard and goatee. Michael was in the enormous photo room when I finally came strolling in.

I shook off all the fucked up thoughts that seem to take up residency in my brain, and got into work mode. I put on my game face, ran my hand across my forehead and got down to what I do.

"Hello, my name is Dana Jackson. Please to meet you; I'll be your photographer today."

The couple that stood before me were very chipper and ready to have their memories immortalized.

HE THOUGHT HE HAD ME

Michael handed the forms to me that the couple had filled out, letting me know what kind of package they were going with. I looked at the couple who was showing so much love and admiration for one another that I was about to lose it.

Hearing the couple mention that they were married thirty-three years made me wonder, will I ever have a love so special, so grand that pain no longer exist in my heart.

The couple got behind the Chinese silk screen, undressed and prepared for their nude optics to be taken. Michael positioned them on the bed and made sure the light was just right. I nodded my head letting Michael know that everything was on point.

I was happy to see that the couple had quite nice bodies to be in there sixties, but getting paid three grand for pictures; I could care less on how their bodies looked. Most of the time couples were so damn happy to see themselves in such a different light that they forgot all about being naked.

After about a dozen pictures they finally decided on the perfect one. I wanted to just pick one for them, but I had to realize that I was just frustrated from earlier.

After they picked their pictures and I ran through client after client, it was damn near 9p.m. The room was covered will all sorts of camera equipment and back drops. I decided to tell

Michael that I would put some of this shit away; hell it's not like I was in a hurry to get home.

"Dana you know that's what you pay me for. Why you trying to do it all huh?" Michael said, in his smooth velvet voice. It did bring a half smile to my face though.

"I know Mike, but we had a lot of photos today. Your tired just like I am, so we may as well help each other so we both can get out of here sooner rather than later."

I went to the closet to store the old film and took a quick inventory for restocking.

Michael walked up behind me, he must saw that I was troubled by something because he ran his hands across my shoulders which caused me to jump slightly and turn around and face him.

"What's wrong Dana?"

"You know Mike, we took pictures of every kind of rich person today, and to have all the money you want and not have to need anything is a wonderful thing."

Dana leaned up against the door with her head hung low.

"What you tripping for? You're gonna be right up there with the rich and famous folks you snap pictures of. You watch what I tell you, and you not doing too bad your damn self. You live in a condo, drive a Mercedes Benz, and you're always dressed to the nines; so what are you saying?"

I looked up at him briefly and realized that most of my problem isn't within my career, it's actually with Marques masking my pain; something I was good at.

"I started this photography stuff when I was nineteen years old, and that's all I ever wanted to do. Therefore, when I graduated from high school, I started *Dana's Looks* out of my studio apartment. It really didn't take off until about eight years ago. Trust there was nobody trying to get their pictures taken by a so called non-professional, especially when all the big names are in magazines and doing run way shows."

Michael walked a little closer to me, as if he was about to tell me something he didn't want anyone else to hear.

"But you're doing it Dana. Most people have a dream and not one clue on how to make it come true; but you living yours."

"Thanks Michael, you know I had to step my game up so I started taking nude photos. I started taking pictures of the freaky folks in the neighborhood, ashy asses and all. Then when they wanted me to start taking coochie pics, I just knew I had to up the price; and I must say it has worked thus far."

The whole time I spoke, Michael stared at me like he was a fox and I was the damn hen.

HE THOUGHT HE HAD ME

Every time I walked away from him, I could feel his eyes on my ass. I can't lie, I made sure I switched just a little harder. I know it was wrong but hell if he looking; I'm switching.

The words "I'm going down" rang through my phone. I reached in my back pocket and pulled out my phone.

"Hello."

"Yeah, where are you at?"

Marques is really acting like he got an attitude and shit.

"I'm about to leave work. Where the hell are you?"

"I'm out here on the grind, you know what I do Dee."

"Yeah I do. I wasn't referring to any damn street shit either, more like women and pussy. Well is it safe to assume that you're coming home tonight?"

"I pay the damn bills there, don't I?"

"Please don't get it twisted. We both pay the bills, but hey if you say so."

I started walking back to the photo room so I could leave and saw that Michael was sitting at the photo table looking at some negatives.

"Look Dee, I won't be home until late tonight; maybe three."

HE THOUGHT HE HAD ME

"Did you just say three in the fucking morning Marques? I damn sho' hope you don't think that I'm going to sit up and wait on you?"

I started yelling before I could catch myself. Michael looked my way briefly then held his head back down.

"What the fuck is that supposed to mean Dee? You usually do, what you got something better to do?"

All the while I was on the phone arguing with Marques ass, I could see Michael getting ready to head for the front door. He was standing in the front of the glass door, clearly waiting on me to finish my conversation. I was done with Marques ass tonight.

I cut the lights off and cut the alarm on and let Marques walk me to my car. I saw him walk to his car. I drove up on him, I was shocked to see him pushing a nice whip as well.

"Mike, is this you cruising around in a pearl black Lexus?"

I don't think I've ever seen what kind of car he drives. Most of the time I'm always on the phone arguing with Marques to even notice.

"Yeah you know how I do."

"Shit I do now!"

HE THOUGHT HE HAD ME

Mike was about to step in his car before he turned and looked at me.

"Dana would you like to go get a drink? After the long ass day we have had, I can't help but notice that you could use one. And for goodness sake, it's Friday night and it's only ten."

Lord knows I didn't want to hurt his feelings and I damn sho' don't mix business with pleasure. The gesture was nice, but this wasn't about to happen.

"Awe Mike, thanks love but I have plans already. Can I take a rain check and we possibly do this next week?"

It was a lie. I'm knowing damn well, he and I aren't about to go and have no damn drinks, but I figured it will saved me sometime until he asked again.

Michael tilted his head to the side, not being pleased with what I just said. He gave me the fake smile anyway.

"I totally understand. This was last minute anyway. Have a safe and good night beautiful."

Damn, on the right day, New Years; he could possibly get it. Which means then, he would have to quit or I fire his ass. Then I would have to get another assistant. Either way this wasn't sounding like anything I wanted to tap into. Since it's Friday, I was headed to meet Alana at one of her favorite spots.

HE THOUGHT HE HAD ME

I finally made it home, walking through my spacious home decorated with African paintings and sculptures. I headed up the stairs to my master bedroom, passing the two other bedrooms I had, that no one occupied.

I really didn't need a three bedroom home. I hoped in the last three years he and I would have made a baby within all this time. Maybe it's for the best. Who the hell would want to bring a baby into this bullshit of a mess?

My phone started singing again, *I'm going down.* I hesitated to answer knowing he was calling with some bullshit.

"Hello," I answered, the phone with an attitude.

"You home yet?"

"Marques, of course I am. Where else would I be?"

I sat down on the chaise longue at the end of my bed, taking off my shoes.

"I'm wrapping things up out here and I'll see you later...one."

The phone click off and I was still holding it like I didn't actually hearing a dial tone in my ear. I hated that he always said he was coming home in the wee hours in the morning, then called and say he would be home sooner rather than later. I believe he just trying to make sure my ass is really home. One day I'm going to surprise him and then we'll see how that shit pans out.

I went to run my shower, to wash Marques and his bullshit down the drain. Once in, I let the warm water cascade over my body. There were vanilla and lavender scented candles lit around the bathroom in various corners of the vanity table. The shimmer from the flicking light of the candles were helping the mood of lust and passion fill the room.

I barely heard the chime from the door, but I knew his ass was finally home.

Marques walked straight in the steam filled bathroom. I caught an eerie feeling that someone was watching me and just as I slowly turned around, he was standing there and watching me through the glass doors.

I raised my arms up over head so he could get and eagles eye of my neatly trimmed "V" and firm supple breast. His ass got undressed in record time and slid inside the shower with me. Moments like this I absolutely love.

"Damn you gotta fat ass baby."

Just like a nigga thinking they can come in and fix everything with sex.

As ready as I was to ignore his ass, I was so damn happy that he was here. I just wish he finally get his shit together.

HE THOUGHT HE HAD ME

Marques started rubbing on my ass and kissing me gently on the neck. This was a good way to loosen me up from the tension he knew he has caused. Letting the water fall over our bodies I couldn't help but remember when I fell in love with him.

****

I met his ass at a chicken and rib joint on the Westside of Chicago, I was not impressed with his so called swag. Hell, I see shit like this every day, but he did have that tall, medium build. He sported a Caesar haircut, and from what I can see he was tatted. He had tats on his neck and forearm, so I assumed his back and chest was tatted as well. He rocked a pair dark blue Levis, a tee-shirt and a pair of royal blue chucks. I can definitely say this man was fine to me.

All I could do while standing there was think...Don't get moist! At a quick glance we locked eyes and he introduced his self.

"Hey beautiful, I'm Marques."

I didn't want to be rude and not give out my name but I felt compelled to give him my real name or maybe it was my pussy talking.

"Hey, I'm Dana."

"Very pretty name. Aye you got a man?"

I started to smile hard; him being straight forward made my inside turn over.

"In fact I don't have a man. Do you have a woman?"

I know he didn't think he was gonnna ask me who I'm fucking, and I wasn't asking him the same damn thing.

Number 8 was yelled from behind the bulletproof glass. I stepped up to the window to pay for my food. Marques looked at me.

"I got this ma."

I hope he don't think he just did something paying for a dinner that was only $8.70

"Thank you, you really didn't have to do this."

"That's the beauty in it ma, cause I know I didn't have to."

Hell I couldn't do shit but smile, grab my food and head for the door.

"Aye ma! Can I get a number or something?"

HE THOUGHT HE HAD ME

I can tell he wasn't about to let this moment pass him by and I was elated that he asked. He pulled a piece of paper from the menu in the window; I jotted down my cell number.

"Don't wait too long to use it."

"You're my kind of girl."

He was now smiling a sexy smile I might add.

After hopping in the car and driving home, I couldn't help but think about dude during the 15 minute drive; which only made me want him sooner rather than later.

I didn't even bother with the food I had just thrown on the kitchen table. I went to the bathroom to run me a hot shower and look in the wall cabinet where I kept all my goodies.

I had a jack-rabbit, the bullet and my favorite 12 inches of thick black love. A woman can't get full on plastic and silicon alone, she must have the real deal at some point and I think meeting Mr. Marques will let me test that theory.

HE THOUGHT HE HAD ME

Alana

Here we go again; listening to this damn alarm makes me want to throw it out the window. Out of all the jobs I could have been doing, I went for the most time consuming job...an Obstetrician.

My pay is through the roof but the hours are long. I gotta let go of this bed but I damn sure don't want to, especially looking at this fine specimen of a man lying next to me.

Before I could even get the covers off of my naked body so I could get ready for work, I feel Edward's hands glide across my voluptuous breast, rolling each nipple between his thumb and pointer finger. The touch of his hands sent chills over my body which harden my nipples, making them hurt just a little.

A soft moan escaped my lips, he does this shit every morning and like a kid in a candy store I get all excited and shit.

"Morning baby," his deep voice mesmerized me.

"Good morning my love. You know I have to go to work. So why do you do this to me each and every morning?"

I couldn't help but smirk as I spoke, knowing I didn't want any of this to stop.

"Well if I didn't, then I would have to worry about who is."

HE THOUGHT HE HAD ME

Edward made sure I was fulfilled as much as he could. The thought of another man fucking his woman, wasn't a thought he wanted entered into his brain.

"You know you are the only one for me baby," I said in a very tranquil voice.

"And that's why I fuck you good each and every morning before we leave so you won't forget."

He said that with much base in his voice, not that he needed to add any; but he did want to make sure he got his point across.

At the very moment he said that, I knew I was going to be late for work; yet again. There wasn't always time for our one-hour four-play sessions. So being the woman that I am, and knowing that his dick is a hard as a sewer top; I'm about to ride this mothafucka into the sunset...sort of speak.

We fight to see who gonna take the lead. Once he finds me mounted on him, he had no choice but to lay there and take this pussy the way it was about to be served.

Leaning in to kiss him passionately, tasting his tongue, sucking his tongue, feeling him grab my head and push my mouth deeper into his, so his tongue could assault my mouth. Deep moans escaped us filling the room with impending sex session.

HE THOUGHT HE HAD ME

"Shit Alana! I feel the heat from your pussy. I feel like you're about to melt into me and stay forever."

Hearing him say that was music to my ears also music to my hips.

As I started to grind my hips, letting the friction between his boxers and my panties ignite a fire that couldn't be contained, Edward slid his hands over my back and then down to my ass sliding his finger up and down the crack of my ass; knowing how much I love ass-play.

Using his hands to slide my panties off, raising one leg at a time to take each leg out, he lifted his body to pull his boxers off. My body shuttered just feeling that hard ass dick underneath my wet, plump pussy that was ready to be dicked down.

Breaking our many kisses to look into each other eyes as I reach down, lifted my body slightly to position, so I could slide down his awaiting dick to feel up my insides.

"Yes that's it baby; ease that pussy down on me."

Watching him bite his bottom lip and close his eyes made me all that more horny. While resting on my knees I rocked back and forth in a slow motion gaining momentum with every rock of my hips. Sitting straight up, letting him palm and caress my breast and roll each nipple between his fingers.

HE THOUGHT HE HAD ME

"That's it baby fuck your man, shit fuck your man."

I knew hearing that, it was time to put in some real work. I leaned forward on his chest, while he wrapped his arms around my back holding me tightly. I started licking on his ear and trialing my way to his neck, making my little marks along the way. I propped this ass up and tightened this pussy. All that was being heard was the slapping of wet skin and moans bouncing off the walls.

"This is your pussy baby. You like this pussy? You like the way I'm fucking you?"

Knowing exactly what his answer would be, I wanted to hear it anyway.

"FUCK! Alana I love this pussy. If I you ever give my pussy to someone else I'll kill your ass. Fuck, don't stop baby. I'm about to cum!"

Did this fool just say what I think he said? I tell you, good pussy will piss off any man but GREAT pussy will have a man planning your damn funeral.

He grabbed my throat with one hand and thrusted deeper into me with ever word he spoke.

"I'm not playing baby, this is MY pussy."

Damn I couldn't do anything but agree. Hell even if I wanted to say different I wasn't ready to die. Feeling him swell inside me, let me know he was seconds away from busting his load of hot tasty cum inside me.

"This shit is coming baby, come with me. FUCK ALANA COME WITH ME!"

I always come on cue when he slamming his dick deep and I'm riding like a champion horse. My clit was engorged and ready to explode.

"Yes that the shit I like baby, us coming together."

Whispering in his ear as he panted away, we both try to regain our normal breathing patterns.

Edward looked me in the eye, "Hey, you're the fucking woman of my dreams and don't you ever forget that."

I heard the words like I have so many times before and I just felt like I was the luckiest woman at that moment.

****

An hour later we both were out the door and ready to start our day. I was in my car and headed in the direction of the hospital, where I'm the head Obstetrician at Northwestern Memorial Hospital. I had to call my girl and see what she was up to; we talk every day no matter what. The phone rang twice before she picked up.

"Heyyy, what up chick?"

"Heyyy Dana boo! What's going on Miss Lady?"

"Shit on my way to the job. What you doing?"

"Hell same as you got a late start though."

As soon as I said that we both fell out laughing.

"I'm sure you did girl."

Dana knew what I meant whenever I said I got a late start, she knew whenever I got the chance to ride my dick, I was gonna do just that.

We continued to make small talk, after arranging to meet at their favorite Jamaican restaurant after work we said our goodbyes. I stepped foot on the 15th floor of the hospital ready to work and get this day over with, until I realized we were understaffed. Which meant only me and three nurses were on the floor, and one of the nurses named Terrell seemed like he would be happiest on Dick Island.

Terrell met me in the lounge area, "Girl are you ready to get to work?"

HE THOUGHT HE HAD ME

I plastered a smile on my face knowing damn well I was pissed off, this was gonna be a long ass day. But I knew at six o'clock, I was getting the hell out of here.

"I guess I am," I said, as dryly as anyone could.

"Well either you gonna sulk or you gonna smile, so which are you gonna do today sunshine?"

Terrell always knew how to make me laugh.

"Alright I will smile today."

"That's more like it boss-lady. Now let me get my charts and get these rooms; see you on the floor."

Terrell was always so damn happy go lucky no matter what, he kept us all cool, calm and collected around here.

"I bet you start holding them damn paychecks till Friday instead of giving them out on Thursday, folks will learn to bring they ass to work,"

Hell Terrell just may be on to something because me staying in any job longer than I need to, just pisses me off by the millisecond.

"I may have to speak to human resources about this shit with these paychecks,"

Terrell looked at me like I had two heads.

HE THOUGHT HE HAD ME

"Human Resources, you're in charge up in here. You give 'em out when you damn well ready. What you need to do is fire those tired, lazy ass chicks and hire some tight ends up in here."

Why the hell does he always have to be so damn dramatic, twisting his lips, waving his hands all in the air, I can really do without all this shit from him, way too damn early for this shit. I swear I'm watching the show, *RuPaul's Drag Race* every time he speaks.

"Terrell your ass is a damn fool,"

Having him around all day, keeps the day moving with much excitement. I always know who fucking who in the hospital, what man is moving from two different rooms because he has two babies on the way. He does keep me informed.

"I wouldn't be if I didn't sprinkle some sunshine on you every day; I truly keep it real," Terrell said, smacking his lips when he finished his statement.

I can say he is about as real as they come. Not like all these fake ass people I work with.

It was time to get down to the nitty- gritty of this work, checking in on patients, doing charts and enduring all the chaos. After hours of being on my feet I knew it wasn't long before I was about to go on break. I told Terrell unless someone was going into active labor not to come looking for me. The day continued at a fast pace there was no letting up, no end in sight.

I had one tough ass sistah that wanted to cuss everybody the fuck out today, because she was having a baby by a man that wasn't there to see the birth of his son. I had to check her ass real quick, we weren't about to be victimized by her verbal abuse. She was either gonna shut the fuck up or deliver this baby on her own. Trust, she shut the fuck up.

After wearing my catcher's mitt through six deliveries I can say in the words of Ice Cube..."Today was a good day."

Even though it was a good day I still had to go toe to toe in a verbal sparring with Terrell ass. All because I slipped up and mentioned that Edward hasn't called all damn day, I won't make that mistake again.

He never lets up, according to him I'm dating Mr. Wrong. I hated getting into my personal business with Terrell, he says he just looking out for me. I say he need to mind his own fucking business.

My day was over and now I was headed on over to meet Dana. When I turned into the already crowded parking lot, I spotted her car.

HE THOUGHT HE HAD ME

The parking lot was crawling with people leaving and meeting up at their cars, like it was an after hour show or something. I walked passed a few people I had known and gave the occasional head nod. I walked into the dimly lit restaurant and saw Dana already waving her hand in the air like she was swatting flies.

I greeted her with a big hug and a kiss on the cheek. I sat across from her and made small talk. As I finish the last of my sentence the waitress came over to take our orders. She was short and curvy, she spoke with a thick Jamaican accent. When speaking to her fellow Jamaicans she spoke Patois, which is primarily an English-African Creole language.

Dana let me order first since she could never make up her mind what she wanted to eat or drink. I ordered the brown stew chicken with a piece of Jamaican bread and a rum punch, I smiled and handed her back my menu.

As usual, the waitress and I were looking at Dana hoping she would be making up her mind soon. Finally, Dana ordered the curry goat with all the fixings and she too ordered a rum punch.

"Denk yuh ladies," the waitress said, while collecting Dana's menu. "Mi ago be bak wid fi yuh drinks."

Dana and I looked at each other not knowing what the waitress was really saying.

"Girl I think she said she bringing our drinks," Dana said, while twisting up her lips.

"Yeah drinks was the only thing I got out of that,"

We laughed knowing that our waitress was gonna speak her native tongue no matter what, we were the ones that were gonna have to catch up.

When the waitress came back she handed us our drinks and let us know that the food would be out in twenty minutes or so. We nodded our heads cause neither one of us was in a hurry to get home.

Dana took a long ass gulp of her drink without the straw, which further lets me know she had some man issues.

"Damn girl, what's going on with you? You wasted no time downing that drink of yours."

Hell, I need to be drinking just as hard as she is, just to stomach this shit she is about to tell me.

"Well for starters he didn't come home the other night. Then last night he didn't come home. He brought his ass home like earlier that morning. I didn't just catch him at his ex-wife house."

I sat there knowing every word Dana was going to speak before she actually said it; these are words I have heard so many times before. Dana was still speaking then stopped just long enough to let the waiter place our food on the table and head back to the kitchen.

"Well what the hell did you do after seeing his ass over there?" I know damn well I would've had a damn shit fit. It's no way I could be so damn calm seeing my man over some other woman house and knowing he's fucking her."

"I did the only thing I could do, after we argued a bit I got in my car and took my ass to work."

I swear I was hoping she was going to say she put his foolish ass out; but no those words never came across her lips. I know one damn thing, I would have to go Bruce Lee on that ex- wife at some point. It's one thing to be sleeping with someone you didn't know had someone else, and then there are the ones that know he got a woman, and just don't care. Oh yeah someone would be getting a welled whooped ass around here.

"Dana how long is this going to go on?"

I looked at Dana, now taking another big gulp of her drink and barely touching her food talking about this bullshit.

"Yeah I hear you Lana."

Now Dana was beginning to sulk.

HE THOUGHT HE HAD ME

"I don't think you do hear me Dana, because if you heard me about a year and a half ago, we wouldn't be sitting here talking about this dumb shit. I don't mean no harm girlfriend, but bullshit ain't nothing but chewed up grass."

I just knew I was going to tell her ass off for having me sit through yet, another one of her ghetto tales about her and this triangle she is in. But it's one thing I know, you can't tell a grown woman who is in love; shit!

We continued our conversation for about another two hours. Half the shit that was coming out of her mouth, I couldn't even believe the shit I was hearing. I know one damn thing; good dick will make some women lose their damn minds. I want to bring her the old Tina Turner album and play, "*What's Love Got To Do With It*," on repeat for her ass.

HE THOUGHT HE HAD ME

Dana

Lying in bed this lazy Saturday morning, Marques decided to get up and out early. So, I'm in need of girl time with my bestie Alana. I bet having my ass out all night will piss him off once he realizes that I've been gone all damn day. I'm gonna make sure that I don't even ring his fucking phone and if he calls me, he'll simply get the damn voicemail.

I reached over on the black smoked night stand to retrieve my phone so I could call Alana and see if she wanted to hit the streets with me today. I punched in her number and waited for her to answer.

"Hello."

"Why the hell do you always do that when you see me calling your damn phone? Just say hey Dana or sis, but that damn dry ass hello is a no-no."

That shit irritated me every time she did that. Why the fuck would she say hello when clearly, my name popped up on her phone.

"Well damn! Next time I won't try and be so damn polite. And what the fuck has your attitude on shit this morning?"

HE THOUGHT HE HAD ME

I wasn't in the mood to hear this shit from Dana this morning. At the very least, let me get my damn coffee before she start in on her and that man of hers.

"Nothing, except when I got up Marques ass was up and gone already. Of course when we talk about it he'll say he had business, but we both know what kind of business he had."

I knew Alana face was all screwed and she was probably shaking her head right about now.

"Well as you know I'm over here shaking my damn head but we will not dwell on this shit today. It's the end of August and we're going to get out and enjoy this day. And I'm sure you're probably going to want to go shopping in those high priced ass stores, that anyone one over the size of a twelve, can't fit shit anyway."

I swear Dana's ass always dragging me to this blow up doll size ass stores and I always leave out with some lotion, or earrings. This shit blows me every time.

"I know damn well you are not tripping on prices Ms. Obstetrician."

"You know what I mean Dana."

"Come on Alana, it is the end of summer sale and I don't want to miss it. Look you hollering in my ear over clothes that I can't fit, won't make me move any damn faster."

HE THOUGHT HE HAD ME

"Oh damn Alana! Don't start this shit with me. You got all the ass I want to have," Dana said, while she continued to talk and express her dislike of shopping with me.

I began moving around my bedroom, letting my feet sink into the plush carpet that comforted my toes.

"Well you can have the thighs, hips, legs, arms, and stomach as well."

Yeah when she heard that I bet she won't be jumping at the chance to get any of those things. I remember saying I was going to get slim for the summer, hell that was in the beginning of January; guess I'll shoot for the holidays.

"Okay Alana, can you please be ready within the hour so we can just go out and hang, and do some girl shit. I'm not sitting up in this house today."

Alana agreed to have herself ready, which I knew was a lie and she would need at least two hours.

Clicking the phone off, I saw I had a missed call and I didn't even hear my phone go off. That damn Alana getting me upset listening to her rant and rave about her not fitting this or that.

It was Marques ass I had missed a call from. I was reluctant on calling him back, I'm going to make this conversation as fast as possible. Looking through my call log I pushed the miss call I had and listened to the phone ring three times before he decided to pick up.

"Dana I've been calling you. Where the fuck are you at?"

I knew this was gonna be one of those bullshit ass conversations.

"I'm at home getting ready to go meet Alana for a girl's day and night out."

"OH! Let me get this shit right. You'd rather be out with your girl instead of spending free time with your man."

This Negro has straight got me fucked up right about now.

"First off it is Saturday,"

I can't believe his ass cut me off mid sentence.

"And what the fuck does that got to do with anything Dee?"

"Well if you hadn't cut me off I could've finished. Like I was saying it's Saturday and you usually play ball, but if you had said something this morning before just leaving, we could've spent some time together, and you would've known that I was going out today."

"You know damn well you are suppose to call me before you decide to go anywhere, and I don't even like you spending time with that bitch especially while you out spending money!"

HE THOUGHT HE HAD ME

This damn fool has lost his entire fucking mind I see.

"First it's my money I'm spending. What business is it of yours what the hell I do?"

I was fired up now.

"Your money; not when you always got your fucking hand out asking me for hundreds here and there, hell sometimes you ask for a thousand and like a dumb ass I give it."

"Oh, so you supposed to be a dumb ass for giving your woman money? Aint that a bitch!"

I'll never, ever tell him how much money I make. So no matter what he doing out in those streets he has no choice but to bring me my cut. I bet that bitch Shawna ain't getting shit, other than a wet ass.

"All I know is, at this very fucking moment you got the wrong one Dee,"

I knew just by the way he talked, I knew his eyes was slanted, his teeth closed tight, and that major vein popping out in the middle of his forehead; he was pissed.

"I got somewhere to be, so when you calm down feel free to call me back."

HE THOUGHT HE HAD ME

I knew I was gonna have to deal with this shit later on tonight, but I damn sho wasn't gonna deal with it right this moment.

I threw my phone on the bed; he knows how to piss me off so fucking bad. I grabbed my white booty shorts and slid them one and let the cuff hit right under my ass cheeks. I wore a black wife beater and let my perky double D's show off some clevage, and put on a satin black tie, a black fedora, and black wedge shoes. I always wear my hair in a short crop-do; nails and feet stay hooked up too.

I checked myself in the full length mirror in the hall and knew right then and there as many chances as I have given Marques; I knew his time was running out with me.

HE THOUGHT HE HAD ME

Alana

This fucking girl is driving me insane and I don't think she knows she's really doing it, but then again; hell her ass knows. She wants to drag my ass all up and down Michigan Avenue popping in store to store.

All I could do was swing my legs out of bed and checked my phone to see if Edward had called; but of course he hadn't. These business trips he takes be on some straight bullshit! And why the fuck can't I ever go with him? Granted I don't want to sit through no type of Real-estate seminars, but at least we could be together. I may just have to look into this.

Trying to figure out what I'm wearing on this warm sunny day, I started to reflect on the things I have come to have throughout my career. I went to medical school because I was not gonna be dependent on a man for nothing, other than his dick. I never wanted to worry about where I was going to live or how I was gonna eat.

I saw a lot of women with high hopes while I was in college. Especially this one girl, I just knew she was gonna be one of the biggest, killer lawyers in Chicago. But she fucked around and got with this loser name Victor. She met him around campus selling his underground CD and she thought she had hit a

HE THOUGHT HE HAD ME

fucking gold mine. She wanted to be something in life but instead she held on to his coat-tail and got nothing.

I walk into this closet and I never know what to wear. I have enough clothes to could dress a whole damn football field of folks with shoes and boots to match, and yet I don't know what to wear. I know I need to find something to squeeze this size 16 in and for all of you that don't know that's weight of 240lbs. Shit I love my collard greens and corn bread thighs I just want a smaller portion of them.

Standing 5'4, light skinned, full breast, round face, and cute dimples, I have heard I have the most mesmerizing eyes any man has seen. No they are not of a fancy color, they just speak to you if you're listening.

Fuck it, I'm gonna settle on my black skinny jean capris, my ruffled red tank top and I'll definitely wear my red bottom flats. Hell I can still be cute with flats on. I know her ass gonna show-up in some heels higher than her ass to walk around the mall, that shit makes no sense to me.

After showering and getting dressed, I popped my red, black and green African earrings in my ears and seeing that my braids where nice and neat, I was ready to go; just waiting on her slow poke ass.

I had a little time to kill so I decided to call my hunny. I plopped down on my red leather wrap around sofa dialing his number with one hand and surfing the channels with the remote in the other hand. After three rings he finally answered in his baritone voice.

"Hey my love."

I love when he says stuff like that.

"Hey my love."

Calling each other the same thing was corny to some but awesome to us, as he is mines and I am his.

"I'm so damn glad you called me. I'm having a fucked up day already and it's just going on noon."

"Talk to me. Tell me what's wrong."

I hated when he had bad days. At least if he was here I would fuck that stress out of him, but I guess that will have to wait until he comes back home.

"I have a client who is about to purchase a thirty-million dollar home from me and he has not received the blue prints for some remodeling he wants to do. If he doesn't get them, he's moving on. Hold on my love, Monica my assistant just let me know I have another call. Hold on don't go nowhere."

When he answered his call I just thought about how frustrating he must feel and I feel helpless right now. Within a few minutes he was back.

"Yeah baby you there."

"Yes I am. Where was I gonna go? You asked me to hold on."

"True."

"Good news the guy called to say he has received the blue prints and he is pleased. He is a home shopper/buyer for the rich and famous who don't have time to do it themselves."

Finishing up my conversation with Edward he let me know he would be home later on tonight. As I was hanging up, I heard a horn blaring outside my damn house. Dana was only thirty minutes late as usual.

I hopped in her car, she turns to look at me like I had lost my damn mind.

"Um, why the hell can't we take that pretty red Benz you drive? That mutha-fucka does everything except drive for you and yet we still have to take my car."

If this girl don't find something to trip about daily, I truly think she would bust.

"First off, you offered to come get me so that means my damn car stays parked until it's my turn to come get you."

"All I'm saying is that is some bullshit."

HE THOUGHT HE HAD ME

We pulled off laughing at her phony attitude and started our way to the nearest mall. We walked that fucking mall so damn much they could have named a store after us. Dana ass even bout her some flats cause them wedges started tearing her damn feet up. I knew better, always flats when there is a lot of walking involved.

At 9 o'clock, Dana was dropping me off back at home and I knew Edward was gonna be home soon. We said our good-bys and I made her promise to call me when she got home, but if I know her she is probably about to ride the streets to see if she can find that no good ass nigga she with. Not my problem though.

Edward hadn't made it home which gave me time to put away the clothes I bought and take a shower. Even though I complain about not being able to find nothing that fits, I ran up on this sistah who makes and sells clothes. From the stuff she had in her shop I just knew I had to get her card and purchased two bad ass pant jumpsuits, one red, the other black. Both v-neck halter and form fitting.

I took a step back and looked at them both as I was hanging them up and knew I was gonna rock those. I went into the master bath to run my bath water. I knew I was ready to relax. I poured bath oil and bubbles into my water and began to step out of my clothes, ready to step into the tub when I was caught off guard.

HE THOUGHT HE HAD ME

"Give me that entire ass," Edward said, with his hands palming my ass and smiling.

"Damnit Edward, you scared the shit out of me!"

"I'm sorry sexy-sex, I didn't mean to. I just wanted you to know that I need you now."

He had the look of lust and darkness in his eyes.

As I climbed in the tub he followed right behind me. I felt his eyes burning a hole in my soul. I knew he was looking and admiring every curve on my body.

After he stepped in, he sat and I sat between his legs. That shit didn't last long cause as soon as his hands started caressing my breast and pinching each nipple they became hard as diamonds. I felt him growing in the small of my back all ten and half inches of him was growing and growing.

He pulled my head back to towards his face so he could kiss me and stick his tongue down my throat literally. I turned around in the tub and looked at him; his eyes told me everything his mouth didn't.

He was in the mood for me to ride him. Nothing more nothing less, he needed to let off some steam and I was about to pull that stress right up out of him.

HE THOUGHT HE HAD ME

I mounted him, he slid down just a little so I could be comfortable. I looked down and saw his dick head peeking up from the water, reaching down to keep it steady I slid my pussy down on his shaft. Not taking my eyes off of him, watching him watch me was some sexy shit. He rubbed his hands over my back and my ass.

I rolled my hips slowly and squeeze my pussy muscles. He sucked each one of my nipples in his mouth like it was his favorite mint. I began to roll my hips a little more. He pulled me closer to him and held me tighter kissing all over my neck and lips, sucking in my bottom lip, top lip, back to sucking my tongue, I felt his finger tips knead my skin forcefully.

The more I sped up the rougher he got. He grabbed me by the neck and began choking me, that shit turns me on every fucking time he does it. Water was splashing out the tub onto the floor, water squishing all around in the tub. Our bodies slid across one another, I felt him growing in me, knowing he was about to get that nut he put his hands on my waist and pushed deeper into me with force, I bounced faster until I felt electricity shoot through my body and his hot creamy nut painted my walls.

As we rocked and came together, I was ready for him to remove his dick from my belly and lighten his grip on my neck. We both loved rough sex but I have blacked out from him cummin' and choking me at the same time, so he knows he's not allowed to grab me around my throat during that time. We had grade 'A' sex. There was nothing in the world better than sexing this man of mine.

****

As we stood up and showered, towel drying each other off, I knew I was on my way to bed and I had an early shift in the morning. After using my cinnamon shea butter to moisturize my skin I pulled the covers up and closed my eyes. I heard Edwards phone buzz three times and without even looking in my direction, he actually left the room. So I played possum to hear who the fuck was calling him so damn late at night.

"Why are you calling me?"

"I'm sorry. I thought you were meeting us at Indigos tonight?"

"Well as you can see I'm not getting out tonight, but hey y'all have fun for me."

"Well if that's what you want Edward, but don't give her all the dick; save some for me."

"Will do. Meet me at the office tomorrow for a sample."

HE THOUGHT HE HAD ME

I heard Edward walk back into the room and I even did a light snore to make him think I didn't hear shit. I didn't hear everything but from what I could make out since he could never whisper, he was meeting someone at the office for a sample.

I felt nothing but cool air as the covers was snatched off me and a hard dick was standing right in front of me. He grabbed his dick and started to slow stroke it. "Turn over," was all I heard; of course I did as I was asked.

While Edward was pounding away in my now near sore pussy, all I could do was let a tear fall knowing that I had to pay him a visit at his job. I wonder what samples he giving out and if it's a woman, then I'm simply gonna have to let her know that someone is already riding his dick.

I knew all about his bullshit ass business meetings and Sunday office visits. I play cool and turn a blind eye. Yes I love him, but I'm just waiting until the ball is in my court.

With all the shit Dana tells me about her man, if she only knew half the shit I put up with from Edward, she'd call me the fools of all fools; especially since I'm always riding her about her shit.

HE THOUGHT HE HAD ME

Dana

I'm so fucking and sick and tired of arguing with this bastard till I don't know what the fuck to do.

"Marques how the hell are you gonna get on the phone while I'm talking?"

He told some random bitch he gonna call them back. I don't know who, but I'm sure it was his fucking ex-wife.

"Which one of your bitches were you just talking to?"

"I don't have time for this bitch shit you throwing at me right now Dee."

This nigga around here checking his phone look like he getting shit together; like he about to go somewhere.

"What the fuck you mean you don't have time for this shit? It's your shit we arguing about Marques."

"All I'm saying Dee, is you ain't here for a nigga the way you use to be. When you're out, you don't call and when I'm trying to come home and chill, your ass is always ready for a fucking fight! Or you busy looking at those damn pictures; ignoring the fuck out of me."

HE THOUGHT HE HAD ME

I must have screamed to the top of my fucking lungs, you would have thought someone was being murdered right in the kitchen right in front of me.

"You selfish son of a bitch! Those pictures are my life, it's what I do. I'm a fucking photographer! I take pictures of rich white folks so I can live the life I live in this big ass home alone because you damn sure are never home. I will be damned if I am going to apologize for my fucking success, now if you can't deal with that then that's your fucking problem!"

I was livid. I was seeing red and was ready to put his ass in a body bag.

"All that rah-rah shit ain't bout nothing; point blank period. You know how a nigga feel. I need your undivided attention and you know I ain't not taking no shorts."

The nerve of this muthafucka right here; I almost couldn't believe what I was hearing.

"Well dammit my name isn't Shawna. If she giving you so much attention maybe you should remarry her ass. Oops! You can't; she left you for fucking some bitch in y'all bed!"

"There you go talking that shit again Dee," Marques yelled.

The shit I was yelling; this shit was worst than many of our other fights.

"Whatever Marques if you think I'm gonna keep dealing with this shit you are FUCKING WRONG!"

I was all up on him pointing my fingers in his face, hoping this shit didn't back fire. He grabbed me around my throat and backed me into the wall next to the bedroom door.

"FUCK YOU DEE, IF YOU GONNA STEP THEN STEP BITCH. I DON'T NEED THIS SHIT!"

I watched him as he headed out the door. I was in disbelief, he never called me a bitch before. I heard his truck rev up and heard the tires screeching out the garage. I waited 30 minutes before calling his ass. He answered on the first ring yelling.

"What! I don't have time for you and your shit right now. When I'm done bending blocks, I may come back home so we can hash this shit out, because frankly my patience is wearing thin with your ass."

"You bending blocks or bending other bitches which one is it?"

I heard Marques do a faint laugh over the phone.

"You're really tripping hard tonight ain't you Dee? Maybe you need to call your girl, go do some girl shit I don't know. But if it's anything you know about me, if I'm fucking someone you'll know about it. I have never hid anything from you like that and I'm not about to start. You feel me?"

Before I could say anything I heard the fucking phone click off. This shit has to change and it has to change now.

HE THOUGHT HE HAD ME

Marques

"Come on Vic, let's roll out to K-town. I got a guy out there who has the goods on pills, weed, crack or anything you need. The shit is cheap and it won't leave your ass for dead. So if you wanna roll we gotta get there like yesterday."

I knew my homie Vic was going be on board with this. Out of all my home-boys, I make sure to call him.

"Alright my nigga, let me finish this studio shit and I'm down."

I knew he would be down for this shit.

We hung up and I cruised to his studio spot blazing a blunt, and letting the smoke ignite the neighborhoods I rode through. Thinking back to when me and my homie would be in his momma's basement putting music and shit together. He got that shit and I got my shit. Hell the way I see it, he get his money how he gets it, and I get mines the way I get it. I guarantee no one is going hungry out here in these streets if you fucking with us.

I rode up in front of Vic's spot, and damn if it wasn't mo' pussy standing outside waiting to get a glimpse of him. The shit was like a concert or something. He had his bodyguards standing out front trying to hold down the commotion. Hell I see panties flying through the air. These bitches were definitely on some 'I'm trying to fuck type of shit.' I just know I ain't never hard up on getting no pussy. I get that shit thrown my way daily, but one of these bitches just may get dicked down tonight.

I was about to grab my phone when I saw my boy open the doors and lawd it was pandemonium. He made a quick dash for my truck and I speed off.

"Damn my nigga them bitches want yo' ass."

"That's the shit that come with the territory. I bet I fucked more than half the bitches that was out there. There's nothing I want from an old bitch, but for her to point my ass in the direction of a new bitch with some bomb ass pussy."

We laughed so damn hard, we the kind of niggas that have no love for these bitches out here.

"Damn homie, you living big as fuck I see."

"Hell yeah I am. So when are you gonna stop selling bitches and drugs and take me up on my offer to get this real money?"

This nigga always think someone wants to get in the rap game. It's all good, but I like the shit I do. I make money, he make money.

"Nigga please. I get my money so don't start tripping with this shit."

Vic looked at me like I had said some wrong shit.

"I ain't tripping my nigga you do you, but I'm trying to get you to start buying 30 million dollar ass houses instead of 1.5 million dollar houses."

Vic passed me the second blunt he just finished rolling and I took a long toke off of it. This nigga was starting to blow me, I didn't want to nut up on him but dammit, he was starting to fuck off my evening with all this bullshit he always talking.

Granted he got long money, he a famous ass rapper. I would have to disown him if he didn't have it, and I have long money doing what I do.

I pulled into the spot which was a five bedroom home in the hood that we used as offices, to handle whatever business needed to be handled. We got a few of the youngsters that needed a place to stay with their kids, to provide a damn good cover up. When shit start looking suspicious, all anyone really sees is a woman and her kids living up in here.

We walked into the house and threw our shit on the table. The noise from outside could still be heard inside the house. Vic took a seat in a black leather lounge chair and I walked through the house to make sure all was secure, and no one tried to come up in here.

HE THOUGHT HE HAD ME

In the last room, Tish and her two kids were watching T.V. As bad as I wanted to fuck her, I couldn't; she was on that powder shit. All she wanted was to get high and have a safe place to stay. So I provided all that shit for her, I made sure she did what she needed to do for them damn kids; but I'm telling you she had the phatest ass and the perkiest titties I've seen outside of Dee. She wasn't the best looker, but I knew from the shit I heard in the hood, she got that devastating ass head game.

On my way back from up stairs checking things out, Vic was rolling another blunt while he had one in his mouth, and trying to talk to some chick on the phone. I sat on the leather sofa across from him and started counting money that I had picked up earlier. No sooner than I sit my ass down, he goes on this wanting me to get on the studio and make music with his ass.

"Look my nigga, every time we get together you start on this shit. I'm good. You made your fortune your way and I made mines my way. All I can say is I been pimpin bitches and selling drugs since I was 14 years old. Hell you know this shit and I don't see me stopping."

Vic shook his head taking a toke on the blunt. I continued to count my money as he spoke.

"We both grew up around drugs and hoes. We saw all kinds of shit going on in the hood but…"

Before he could finish I cut his ass off.

"But my ass! We never saw the ones getting money go without lights, gas, phone. They were always eating good and that's the shit I wanted so I got it, while everyone else was eating syrup sandwiches and cold bologna sandwiches; I was eating steak, fried chicken with all the damn fixings and that's how a nigga gon continue to eat, point, blank, period."

"Yeah my nigga, you were always the kind of nigga who wasn't afraid to go to jail. That's why I started rapping, that jail shit wasn't for me." I fell out laughing at his statement.

"Yeah I know, remember when you tried to sell a little weed to buy them new Jordan's, the one Spike Lee did a commercial about. Man when you got caught I thought you where gonna die, but lucky for you I took the rap for that shit. I knew right then and there you where not built for that shit."

I know you got to be built a certain kind of way for this street shit. The streets has been my home for years; I grind hard in these streets.

We finished talking about the past and tried to get some new shit going. Until he asked the one question no man should ever ask another man. But I guess since he know we're both getting money, he felt it was cool.

"So my nigga, how much money you really getting out here doing this pimpin and drug thang?"

I looked him dead in his eye with my blunt hanging out the corner of my damn mouth.

"I could open my own bank my nigga; tax free money."

Vic nodded his head and didn't say shit else. We both knew this conversation was over.

HE THOUGHT HE HAD ME

Edward

"Monica, can you come in here for a moment?"

As usual, my assistant was in here with her pad and pen ready to take down every word or be nosey since she's the one who knows everything about my comings and goings. She walked her fine dark chocolate self in my office and I got an instant hard on.

"I'm ready Mr. McCall."

I looked her up and down with thoughts of lust running through my head. All I could see at this very moment was having her on her knees while I mouth fuck her. I had to quickly shake that shit out of my head.

"First off, I'm going on a three day business trip and I need all my calls to be forward to my cell and fax all documents immediately."

As I talked Monica walked over to the leather chase lounge and had a seat while writing everything down.

"What about Ms. Williamson?" She asked, with a sly smirk on her face.

I knew what it meant and for that very reason I was quickly reminded on why I couldn't fuck her. Alana and everyone would know before the cum dried good.

"What about her? She knows already that I'll be gone and for how long."

I could see the wheels in Monica's head turning as I finished my last statement. She completely stopped writing and seemingly drifted off into space for a moment.

"Okay Mr. McCall, would that be all?"

"Last but not least, I need my suits on the left side of this closet to be packed and have my plane tickets ready for me and I think that would be all."

Monica walked her shapely body out of my office and closed my glass frosted doors behind her.

I walked over to the same walk-in closet I told Monica to get my suits from, and admired all the stuff I have for my late night meetings. I had everything from lotion to hand towels and even that body wash soap that the women love. This office won't smell like pussy when I'm done. I won't go home with the scent of pussy all over my clothes and body. I didn't have this bathroom built with a shower in it for nothing.

HE THOUGHT HE HAD ME

I sat down at my desk and reclined in my chair. I looked at my phone to dial a number, I really didn't want to; but did it anyway.

"Before you say anything come get your ticket and don't be late."

I clicked the phone off. I didn't want to hear shit.

Finally made my way to Miami. Getting off the plane with my suit jacket in my hand and my shades adorning my face, there is no way a woman could resist a man like me. I stand 6'3, body of a gym god, and dark brown skin without an imperfection anywhere. I have dark brown eye color, a bald head, and the most tapered goatee. I dress in the finest of clothes and eat at the finest of restaurants.

I caught a cab to the hotel, checked in, grabbed my room key and headed to the 15th floor. I Dropped my bags at the door, ran a hot shower and began to prepare myself for this small vacation pussy I was about to get.

Before I could get in the shower good, the hotel phone rang. I answered and it was the front desk letting me know I had a visitor. I instructed the lady on the phone to give her a key and send her up. From the back ground noise, my visitor was pissed off.

I hung up the phone and went to take my shower. Twenty minutes later, I emerged from a steamy bathroom and focused my eyes on a 5'3, 120 pounds with curves in all the right places. Her mocha complexion was smooth, and even though she wore green contacts, it made her look all that more seductive. I was a man who had a weakness for the shorties with banging bodies, but that's all those women will ever be is a fuck; nothing more.

"Edward how long are we staying this time?"

I walked over to the bar and made me a drink, rum and coke to be exact.

"Why you got somewhere else to be?"

"No. I was just asking that's all. Damn, why you got to be so snappy with me? I guess that's what happens when you're not getting the right kind of love at home."

I couldn't do nothing but shake my head; women always want to be better than the next one.

"Don't start this shit Trina; you know I get my far share of pussy. As of a matter of fact, I need a catcher's mitt to catch all the pussy that comes my way if you really want to know."

"Well why am I here if you have so many options?"

Trina walked up to me searching for the answer you give a woman you're in love with; instead she got another answer.

HE THOUGHT HE HAD ME

"You're here for two reasons. One, I played any... many... miny... mo, and you got picked. Second you can't keep yo shit to yourself. So don't act like you don't want to be here."

Trina walked back towards the bed, sat down and crossed her legs.

"Alright. Let's not start so soon. Let's just do what we have come to do."

"Now you talking, but first and foremost take a shower."

The look on her face was priceless, as if I had any fucks to give.

"Excuse me. What did you just say?"

"You heard me the first time, so I won't be telling you again."

"Why don't you take one with me?"

"You're not my woman so we won't be playing that damn game; but I'll wait on you."

"Oh you can fuck me like I'm her but you can't take a goddamn shower with me!"

This bitch almost made me drop my damn drink just because of the shit she was spewing at me. She must have lost her fucking mind. Right then and there I walked up to her and the back of my hand was connecting with her mouth; SLAP!

HE THOUGHT HE HAD ME

She fell off the bed and grabbed her mouth with both hands and ran to the bathroom. I refreshed my drink, grabbed my damn phone and called Alana; she picked up after the second ring.

"Hey sexy sex,"

I could hear her snicker, something she did every time I called her that.

"Hey babe, what's going on?"

"Nothing just missing you, and wishing you were here with me. But after this meeting I should be home real soon. It all depends on how they continue to act about the stuff I'm requesting for."

"Well if anyone can get what they want, I know it's you. I'll be counting the minutes until you're home."

I sat on the edge of the king size bed and heard how much she was missing me in her tone.

"Hey sexy sex."

"Yes my love."

"I love you for always."

I didn't even give her a chance to answer; I just disconnected the call.

HE THOUGHT HE HAD ME

Just as I was taking another sip of my drink, a freshly showered Trina walked out the bathroom looking radiant. She walked over to me kissed me and said "I'm sorry."

****

I've always wanted to be with Edward but that wasn't possible since he already had a woman. I do enjoy the time we spent together, no matter what. He can be a bastard at times but I know he loves me and he truly knows I love him. This man looked good, smelled good and dressed exceptionally well.

Watching him sit on the bed I knew, just because my mouth was hurting didn't mean I wasn't about to get some of the best dick I've ever had in my life.

I walked up to him, kneeled down and let him kiss my lips softly. I began caressing his dick with my right hand making sure I kiss him on his neck, chest, and stomach as I worked my way down to his thick dick.

Licking all around the head first so he could feel the warmth from my mouth; locking my eyes on him so he knows he is about to get his soul sucked out of him. Sliding my warm mouth over his dick letting his dick rest on my tongue as is slides to the back of my throat. Holding it at the base until all ten inches is securely in my mouth. The head of his dick is resting in my throat I begin to pulsate and hum causing a vibration. Edward begins to wrap both hands in my hair. His moans are bouncing of the walls, his heavy breathing lets me know he's enjoying every minute of this.

As I slide my mouth back up I make the SLURPPING sound, his dick is covered with thick foamy spit. I pick up the speed and continue to deep throat him, my pussy is literally dripping wet. Sucking Edward's dick always turned me on.

I use both hands and twist them on his dick in opposite directions while I concentrated on the head. At this time he stood up abruptly, moved my hands out the way, grabbed my head and fucked my mouth. His balls were slapping against my chin while he held my head steady. I heard him let out a loud ROAR. His cum painted the inside of my mouth until it was all swallowed. I looked up at him while he was looking down at me.

"You like that daddy?"

All he could do was nod his head yes, his breathing was heavy. I could do nothing but laugh to myself. I don't care what the fuck he thinks he's getting at home, I know damn well he's not getting head like this.

Once he pulled his dick from my mouth, I knew to get into position. Which is on the edge of the bed, head down, ass up.

HE THOUGHT HE HAD ME

Just like he likes it. He didn't want any other position other than this, at all times. Edward was an ass man, he wanted the tightness of a woman's ass and I always made sure he got it.

I felt his masculine hands on the lower part of back pressing down on me. He slid his dick head up and down my pussy to have the head of his dick shining. He brought it up to my ass and I was ready for his penetration. This shit was better than anything I have ever felt.

Edward would fuck the hell out of my pussy but the ass is where it was at for me and him. As he slid the head in, I gripped the sheets. He paused and slid some more in; I clenched my teeth. He slid some more in and I gasped once he was fully in me. He paused so I could get adjusted to the girth and started slowly sliding in and out of me.

I felt his hands on my waist and he started to pick up a little speed, then more speed. I heard him spit on his my ass for more lube. He kept telling me to keep my damn head down and keep my ass up. Getting fucked in my ass was feeling good to me, but when he started pounding harder; that's when I be ready to stop. But not him, and I have to lay there and take the shit; and like a good little woman I do.

He started slapping my ass and holding me tighter. I reached down and started rubbing my clit vigorously, I love when we cum together. Edward let out this bellow that could be heard next door, and let his babies free in my ass.

HE THOUGHT HE HAD ME

I collapsed on the bed, he pulled out and went straight to the bathroom. I wanted to get in the shower with him but knew that wouldn't happen. Both of us had showered, dressed and was ready to have a good time in Miami.

I met him while standing on the street in the Downtown area with my hand stretched out, in a sorry ass attempt to flag down a cab. Every cab either had someone in it or was driving right pass my ass until a black town car pulled up in front of me.

The window slid down and the sexiest looking man, with the smile of a god, wearing the whitest, prettiest teeth I've ever seen asked did I need a ride. Now I knew this was wrong from jump street, but I really didn't give a damn. My brain said no but my pussy instantly said yes, so I jumped in. His words were strong yet soft. He looked at me as if it was lunch time and I was prime rib.

"Thanks you sir for the ride. It has been hell trying to catch a cab in the Chi today."

With every word I spoke my eyes ate his ass up.

"Please, you know my name, don't call me sir."

He smiled and my pussy smiled back.

"Well Edward, since we already know each other's name thanks for the ride."

He cleared his throat before speaking never taking his eyes off of me.

"Nice seeing you again and without your sister this time. Where can I have my driver drop you off beautiful?"

I raised an eyebrow and wanted to see how he would respond to my next statement. He just had to throw my sister in this.

"Anywhere you're going."

He didn't even break a sweat at my statement. I on the other hand almost lost control.

"I am very flattered Trina, but I'm going home to my wife. However I may be persuaded to meet you for drinks at a later date."

Right then and there I told him about this place I knew of that have the bet rum and coke and buffalo wings anyone could want. Then his ass had the nerve to laugh at me.

"I don't usually go to places like that, but I'll try it if you say it's a good spot for relaxing."

"Oh let me guess. You're use to going to places where they call you by your last name and have white linen napkins on the table with a wedge of lemon in your water?"

HE THOUGHT HE HAD ME

Did this fool just act like the shit I like is not to his liking; I guess Mr. stuffy ass need to get a little loose.

"Yes that's where I usually go to unwind but show me what you like and then maybe I'll show you what I like."

His eyes were literally burning a hole in my damn skull. I wanted to ask him to look at something else but felt good at the same time that he kept his focus on me.

He reached in his jacket pocket and gave me his card that had his cell number on it. I knew I was using this damn thing real soon.

"Thanks for the card. I'll put it to good use but for now this is my stop."

He looked out the window to search his surroundings and saw I was getting out at Michigan and Chicago Ave.

"Looks like someone is going shopping or something. Remember to put that card to use beautiful."

I looked at him one last time before the driver opened the door, winked and didn't say a word. I made sure he got a good glimpse of this ass before I exited the car. I went on about my business shopping and smiling the entire time knowing I was about to get some of that dick sooner rather than later.

HE THOUGHT HE HAD ME

Three weeks later, I called his ass. He even remembered who I was. He says he never forget beautiful women, I believe it was his tactic to insure he would get some pussy. We ended up meeting up at this place called 'Hear Dis.'

He agreed to go hear some open mic stuff with me so we could chop it up. We had plenty drinks and great conversation. He turned out to be a really great guy. We shared little sexy secrets between the two of us that we couldn't share before when I saw him during a party, but we knew tonight was the night we were fucking.

We ended up at the Drake, the night he dropped his pants and that big, black, 10 ½ inch dick with thick veins running up and down it was exposed. I found out that his dick game wasn't shit to fuck with, and I've been hooked on Mr. Edward McCall ever since.

HE THOUGHT HE HAD ME

Alana

I lay in bed. Just as I was about to pull my naked body from the bed, Edward grabbed be around my waist.

"Are you going to work this morning sexy sex?"

I smiled just hearing him say that.

"I was thinking about taking a day or two off since you've been gone for three days. I thought we could spend some time together."

I looked over at Edward waiting on a response. He had a blank stare on his face. I don't know what he was thinking about but whatever it was, it took him far away from here.

After about five minutes Edward seemed to fall out of his trance and finally answered me.

"I'm sorry sexy sex. I have a meeting today with some potential buyers and as you know these are some million dollar deals that I can't pass up."

I knew damn well Edward started sensing my frustration building. I went right on ahead and got my beautiful curvy ass out of bed before I really said something that he wouldn't like. I put my hands on my hips not giving a fuck about titties hanging, belly being exposed; none of that.

"I understand that, but damn can we get together later on tonight?"

I kept a hawk eye on his ass hoping he knew what the fuck he should be saying right...about...now."

"Sexy sex, I have a business meeting with this guy name Byron Davis tonight," Edward sighed, deeply knowing I was trying to figure shit out.

"Didn't his ass just purchase a home from you a few months ago?"

I walked to the bedroom door and grabbed my satin black robe off the back of it letting my ass do an extra jiggle when I walked, just for the hell of it.

"Yeah that's what I'm saying. He's into buying up these mansions and what not. So when he needs or wants a meeting I have to be there."

He got the nerve to be watching my every move and licking his lips. None the less, I know damn well he don't think he about to get any of this BLACK ICE CREAM. I crossed my arms in front of me and walked to the side of the bed he was lying on to continue to ask him questions.

"So what the fuck does this Byron person do for a living since he's buying up million dollar homes and what not?"

HE THOUGHT HE HAD ME

Edward took a deep breath yet again and rubbed his hands down his face. He looked at me hoping I wouldn't keep asking questions.

"He manages his nephews rap career. I don't give two fucks what he does for a living as long as he spending that money. shit I'll go on meetings as much as I need to. And I hope that you being my wife will understand that. Look at it this way that means more money for us so I can keep your fine ass in diamonds and gold."

Edward has flung the covers off his naked bottom in an attempt to seem pissed off which I didn't give a fuck. I can buy my own diamonds and gold. This negro has lost his damn mind if he thinks for one moment that I'm impressed with that kind of shit. It's like every time I want to do something he busy and shit. When I start hanging out and doing my thing, I bet he'll changed his tune then. He thought he was gonna make it to the bathroom, thinking that this conversation was over...NOT!

"No. You mean more money for you. I've told you many times before that I had my own shit before you and gonna have it after you, anything else is just a bonus! So please remember who I am and don't forget that shit."

I walked my ass downstairs to the kitchen. I was completely done with this conversation now. How the fuck is he going say some shit like that out of his mouth. I knew he was up stairs getting his shit together to go and do what the fuck ever he had planned for the entire day.

I made me a cup a mud and gathered my thoughts. When I saw him walking down looking like an exact replica of Michael Jai White just taller. This man was so damn fine but fine or not I was pissed. But I knew exactly what to do to rest my mind. I was heading to the city to get the hell out the burbs so I could get my hair and nails done. I already decided to take today off so I may as well put it to some use.

When he walked out the door and without kissing me I knew we were headed for possible trouble.

HE THOUGHT HE HAD ME

Dana

"Marques this is our last and final fight. I can't deal with this shit anymore. I don't know what the hell your problem is, but I'm doing everything I know how to do to make us work and you're fighting me every step of the way!"

I was sitting on the leather sofa sobbing in the palms of my hands, hoping that he truly understands me this time. But like everything else, he either makes it all about him or don't hear shit I'm saying. I continued to wipe my tears with the back of my hand. The next thing I knew, he was sitting next to me. He was just letting the wall hold him up. He grabbed my hand when he began to speak.

"Actually Dee, you have done nothing."

He hung his head low and I was on pin and needles wanting to know what the problem was. I spoke softly not wanting to lose this opportunity.

"Marques, well what is it then? Am I missing something?"

"Are you ready to hear what I have to say no matter what it is?"

Now he was beginning to scare the shit out of me. I searched his eyes for clues, but saw none.

HE THOUGHT HE HAD ME

"Hell yeah I'm ready to hear it. Spit that shit out!"

This nigga had the nerve to have me hanging on by a damn thread.

"I need you to do a favor for me Dee, I need you meet this guy for me and make this ten grand for us. My usual girl can't do it but I'm not about to pass up this kind of money. And with an ass like yours I'm sure he'll be pleased."

I wanted to punch the fuck out of him but all I could do was sink into the sofa in disbelief.

"So you want me to turn a fucking trick for you?"

I was hoping I didn't hear him right but I knew what the fuck his answer would be.

"It's not that bad baby. You're always saying you would do anything for me, and I need to make sure that you're on my side."

I couldn't do shit but jump up from the sofa. I was so fucking irate that I couldn't even think straight.

"So you want to pimp me?"

This nigga took of his cap and got comfortable like this was some kind of negotiation. I walked the room back and forth looking for something that makes some kind of sense.

HE THOUGHT HE HAD ME

"Look Dee, I'm gonna say this as sweet as possible. As far as I'm concerned, you're gonna do this. I know how good the pussy is so I know he will too and this nigga bout to spend money for a night of whatever. The ball is in your court, just play the game and the rest is easy."

I couldn't believe my fucking ears I felt like I was about to hyperventilate listening to this bullshit.

"Easy for whom Marques? Damn sure not me!" This muthafucka is taking me through channels that I didn't see coming. I leaned up against the wall where he previous was standing and rubbed my chest my heart felt like it was about to beat out of my fucking chest.

"Look, this is who I am. I've always been this way, I can't change this shit Dee. Sometimes I hate this shit and then there are times that I'm cool with it. No one understands this shit but me and I'm hoping you don't let me down."

This bastard walked his ass over to me and kissed the streaming tears that was glistening my damn face.

Marques was holding me in a tight embrace. I wanted to fuck him up onsite but I just couldn't budge. I was still hoping that he was gonna say this was some bullshit ass joke or something but that never came. The only thing that did come was me feeling his dick growing up against my stomach.

He begins kissing me and whispering shit in my ear.

HE THOUGHT HE HAD ME

"I love you Dee."

I closed my eyes and let him continue to kiss on my tears as they continued to stream down my face, they fell; he wiped. I knew at some point if I went through with this shit, I was going to obliterate his ass at some point.

My body started to writhe in his arms, my sexual appetite was rising and no matter how hard I was trying to fight it, no matter how pissed off I was at this very moment; I knew I wanted his dick in me now.

Our clothes began to decorate the floor. His pants dropped around his ankles and pulled his wife-beater over his head. My full breast was being pulled from my lace bra. He sucked each erect nipple. I wrapped my right leg around his waist, and I reached down to feel his hard dick, ready to slide in the inner recesses of my warm folds.

He forcefully grabbed both breast and pressed them together to lick both nipples. My yoni was sweltering from his touch. Our tongues danced, he turned me around and placed my hands up above my head with one hand, and within one swift motion he was locked inside me.

I started to whimper, but as he sped up I clawed the wall. I couldn't escape the pussy beating he was putting on me. He had his arm around my neck almost in a full choke hold, he pounded away. I screamed out in pain but that never stops him, it makes him go harder.

His grip around my neck got tighter by the second; he exploded inside me while he kept me pinned to the wall. He let out a loud grunting noise as he continued to empty his seeds inside of me. We both were breathing heavy. He kissed me on my back and back of my neck, then whispered in my ear.

"Are you gonna do it for me?"

I let out a deep sigh.

"I'll do it, just keep me safe baby."

I hated the moment the words left my fucking lips; I felt instantly sick on the stomach.

"I'll never let anything happen to you. You're my woman."

This was so fucked up, now I'm letting this man pimp me. This can't be the way love goes.

HE THOUGHT HE HAD ME

Marques

Rolling over at six in the morning, I watched Marques sleep. He was turned facing me so I gently kissed his lips. I went to the bathroom and thought about how he fucked me up against the wall. If I don't know anything else, that man can fuck like nobody I've ever been with.

I did my morning rituals while in the bathroom.

I expected to see Marques still laying in bed. It was still early but I knew if he wanted to have sex this morning, I wasn't about to be kissing him with morning breath. When I came back to the room he was sitting up in bed with the remote in one hand and his phone in the other.

"Why are you up so early babe?"

I was shocked to see him sitting up in the bed, I didn't like where this could go because it is always something with him.

"I was waiting on you to come out the bathroom. I just wanted to make sure you were still okay with everything we talked about yesterday."

Damn it's too damn early for this shit, I can't believe this. I walked over and got into bed just as naked as I got out of it. I pulled the covers up over my legs, hoping that the exposure of my bare breast would get his attention enough to drop this conversation. He looked my way only for a brief second, to get a clarification on how I was feeling about this whole pimpin' me shit.

"Marques I told you I'm on your team. But why do we have to discuss this so early in the morning?"

This was the last thing I wanted to hear this morning. We're both sitting up in the bed pretending to watch television. I pulled the covers up over my entire body at this time. He surely wasn't checking for me at this moment.

"We gotta talk about this. I have a guy lined up and I need to get things in order. "

He looked at me as if I had something to say other than what was being said already.

"Look Marques, I have to be at work at ten and you're about to fuck my head up for that. I'm not about to deal with this shit right now."

I was done with this conversation.

Marques jumped his ass out of bed dick swinging and all. He grabbed his basketball shorts off the navy blue chaise lounge and put them on. His face was twisted up, his eyebrows met in the middle, I knew he was pissed; but I didn't give a fuck.

HE THOUGHT HE HAD ME

"I don't believe you Dee. I'm fucking your head up? I've always put my shit on the table and let you know what I'm doing. When we first met I would tell you when I fucked some other bitch, when a bitch at the club would suck my dick in the bathroom. Then I told you I pimp hoes, sold drugs and through all of that you stayed, but now when I need you, my fucking woman, you freeze up on me!"

As he talked he walked from one end of the room to the next slapping his fist in the palm of his other hand.

"I am not freezing up on you. All I said was I don't want to talk about this so damn early in the morning."

I was on ten, this muthafucka don't know when to let up unless he about to get his way; then he'll shut the fuck up.

"Fine Dee, but at some point we'll be discussing this shit in full detail."

He grabbed his black robe and went into the bathroom, leaving me feeling like he just pissed on me and gave me a dirty ass towel to wipe myself off with.

I heard the shower running, I knew he was about to get ghost on me. I jumped my ass up, went to the downstairs bathroom, showered and dressed in record time. Knowing him, he thought I'd be in the kitchen fixing the breakfast he never eats. But I had one better for his ass, I left the house without telling him. I left an hour earlier than I normally do but I knew I had to get the fuck out of the house and away from him.

As I was getting into my car my phone rang, I pushed the button on my Bluetooth and told my mom, "Good Morning."

We talked all the way until I got to work. With it being the beginning of fall, she wants me to come to Atlanta for the holidays. I'm not sure if that's what I want to do, but it'll give me something to do instead of sitting here with Marques ass fussing, cussing and fighting damn near every day.

The more I thought about it, I knew my mind was damn near made up; I was taking my ass home for a while. I didn't want to tell momma just yet, she would never let me rest until she actually saw me walk through her door.

For now I'll keep it to myself. I asked her did she need anything and like normal she said her usual line, "Baby Lou I just want you to come home." Every time I heard her say that, I knew I could always find comfort at home.

I wrote a check out for five thousand dollars to send to mama. She didn't say she needed it, but like my mama knows me; I know my mama.

****

If Dee think I'm about to sit up worrying about her and this bullshit, she crazy as fuck. I said what I have to say. I just know that when I say something, come hell or high water it's gonna get done, and like many times before 'D' knows she don't want these problems with me. I can be a nice guy or I can become the devil. I hope baby chooses wisely.

I noticed her ass left quick as hell. I hope she knows that don't mean shit to me, as long as she knows what team she plays for I could care less. The only thing I care about is money. That's it, that's all.

I finished getting dressed and grabbed the fresh pair of Air Force Ones out of the closet. I wore dark grey Levis with a white-tee. Threw ice on my wrist and neck and let the smell of Invictus cologne drive these women crazy when I walk pass.

I grabbed my phone before I was about to push out the door and called my man Vic. I needed him to ride with me for a quick minute. I hope he wasn't going to be acting like a fucking bitch. After the second ring he picked up.

"What up my nigga? I need you to ride out to K-town with me, won't take more than an hour or so."

I waited for his response which I knew was going to be some bullshit.

"What up man? I'm here at the studio about to lay these vocals down, gotta catch you next time my nig."

"Damn man, I just need another pair of eyes that's all."

HE THOUGHT HE HAD ME

"Can't man. I got other people in the studio ready to lay down their vocals. I can't leave my people like that."

This nigga always pulled this I'm at the studio shit. I believe he was scared to roll out in K-town with me. I can't stand a pussy ass muthafucka.

"Fuck it then. I swear when a nigga doing them you never wanna roll, but you always trying to get someone to come to the damn studio with your ass. This my last time asking you for shit."

"Damn my nigga, it ain't even like that. But I tell you what, when you tired of all this pimpin and slanging come holla at your boy. I always got a spot on my team for you my nigga. You feel me?"

Dis nigga think I need a fucking hand out, he must be one stupid muthafucka.

"It's cool, I got this my nig. I'll holla back. One"

I hit the Stevenson expressway and made my way to the Westside. Cruising alone I saw a few of my big booty loves handling their business. I knew one thing was for damn sure, these hoes were loyal. I mean they come on their period or have a baby, they still sucking dick and taking it up the ass.

I was out here bending blocks doing my usual get down, making sure everyone was good and no problems were on the rise. I saw my girl KeKe walking, staggering out the alley. Before I could say anything, she ran up to me and laid two grand in my hand.

She was high as fuck, knowing her she just popped a molly. I had to let her know that I was a girl short and she needed her to be out here a little while longer; she didn't mind at all.

I could've told that bitch to go fuck in Lincoln Park Zoo and she would have. Keke's only concern was making sure I had my money in my hand and on time. I didn't play that its late shit cause if that shit happened, it was a beating to the tenth power on their ass.

I hopped in my truck and pulled from the curb. When I got to the corner I saw one of my special girls. Tay was sitting on a stoop hunched over. Her clothes was torn off, her lip was busted and her hair looked like a birds nest.

I threw the truck in park and jumped out. Walking up to Tay, I was getting pissed by the second.

"Tay! Tay!"

She slowly lifted her head and tried seeing me through squinted eyes.

"Oh hey daddy."

She looked fucked up.

HE THOUGHT HE HAD ME

"Who did this shit to you Tay?"

She was trying to stand but kept staggering like a muthafucka. She was high as hell; that crack has truly fucked her up.

"It was that nigga Jimmy that be fucking with all us hoes out here. He had money for some head but wanted some ass too and I refused so he hit me."

My insides were burning the fuck up. I knew it was time to pay Jimmy punk ass a visit.

"I got one question Tay, do you have my money?"

I had to keep shaking off the images of my once beautiful sister. After she got gang raped she was never the same. She got on drugs to numb the pain and this has been her life since she was twenty-two. She pulled my money from inside an old flower pot and handed it to me with a smile.

"Don't worry daddy, I always got your money."

I hated when she called me that.

"Tay, please stop calling me that. I've told you that already, damn! I'm about to take you to the spot so you can get cleaned up, get some rest, eat and what not. But I'm going to need you out here tomorrow. You feel me?"

"Yeah daddy, I got you."

HE THOUGHT HE HAD ME

I helped her in the truck and took her to the spot. I couldn't even look at her. I don't give a damn, I'd rather her sell her ass for me than some nigga I gotta fucking kill for putting their damn hands on her.

I dropped her ass off and paid Jimmy ass a visit, he was never hard to find.

I let him know when I did see him that he could finally join the team. He was all too happy to hear that, since that's all he ever wanted to talk about when I saw him. He was always letting me know how he would put in work whenever I needed him too. I told him that we needed to take a ride; it was his last ride.

The garbage men found his ass the next morning.

HE THOUGHT HE HAD ME

Alana

Sometimes you just gotta get out and hang with your girls. Since I didn't have to go to work, I hit my girls up from the city and got caught up on some much needed hood gossip at the beauty shop.

I was getting my hair laid and with all the trimmings including nails and feet. My stylist Jazzie was on point with the hair though. She was a chocolate petite beauty, she only stood 5'2" her bark was indeed bigger than her bite but she made you think she would tear you a whole new ass hole. Jazzie sensed something was wrong I guessed I "sighed" too many damn times and not even realized it.

"What's up girl? I'm sitting here doing your nails and we're supposed to be catching up but your mind is a million miles away. What's on your mind?"

I didn't want to tell her, even though she my girl she can get a little loose with her lips during beauty shop talk. And I damn sho don't want my business to be the latest gossip around town.

"I have man trouble that's all,"

I wanted to make it simple and hope she didn't read too much into it but as normal she did.

"Hell we all got them problems, but as fine as your man is... I mean no disrespect but damn he fine! I don't see what you got to be tripping on; you live in the burbs, got a phat ass house and drive the most banging ass car. What's the problem again?"

This is why I didn't want to say nothing. My girl only see the material shit and not the meaningful shit that a relationship is suppose to bring.

"Yeah, well all I'm gon' say for now is, all that looks good ain't good."

I watched her hang on my every word like she was about to get the winning lottery numbers; but I was done with this conversation.

"Well you know me. Just call me Jazzie the spy. I specialize in spyology, when and if you need me I got your back."

I knew between her and Dana they would have my back got to keep them on speed dial just in case I need some help one-day.

As Jazzie finished my manicure and pedicure then my hair, we continued to get caught up on all the latest hood gossip. I heard the door chime when a lady came in with a cart full of Soul Food. My mouth instantly started watering at the smell of greens, friend chicken, mac and cheese, and candied yams. I forgot that in the hood you can get anything anywhere.

HE THOUGHT HE HAD ME

I grabbed me a plate and grubbed. Damn I think I miss the hood, can't get this shit in the burbs. I left the beauty shop full of good food and good conversations between old friends. I hopped my ass in my car, took a quick glance at myself in the rearview mirror and thought, "damn I look good."

I dug in my purse and called Edward. I dialed his number but my call went to voice mail. This man must have lost his damn mind! I called his work phone, his secretary Monica answered and connected me to him.

"What's up Alana?"

"Damn you usually call me sexy sex."

I turned my nose up at the phone cause' I heard irritation in his voice.

"What the fuck difference does it make what I call you? But since you did, what do you want?"

This nigga has lost his damn mind. I don't know who or what has pissed him off, but he needs to understand who the fuck I am.

"You know what? Fuck it! I don't have time for your stank ass attitude, especially when I didn't do shit to deserve it! So take your ass back to work!"

HE THOUGHT HE HAD ME

I wasn't about to get into a shouting match with him. I hung up on his ass. At some point, he would find a way to dump this argument in my lap and say it was my fault.

I'm sitting in my car, twenty minutes have passed since I left the beauty shop and all I've managed to accomplish is have an argument with this asshole. My phone started to ring just as I was about to pull away from the curb. I glanced at my phone and saw Edward's picture decorating the front of it. I hesitated in answering but knew I wouldn't hear the end of it if I didn't. I answered but didn't speak.

"I know you're there, so here is what I'm going to do. You can come with me to the meeting tonight, I will text you the address. Just be on time…please."

He hung up and I almost burst at the seams. I wondered what changed his mind but I quickly dismissed that shit. All I know is instead of wondering where I was about to go, it was time to go home and get my shit together.

HE THOUGHT HE HAD ME

Edward

I looked up from my desk and watched Monica stroll into my office just as I hung the phone from Alana. My dick jumped hard watching her cleavage jump out at me and the way her hips was stretching that red skirt she has on, my mind went straight to fucking. When I got off the phone with Alana I couldn't keep my eyes off Monica. I knew exactly what I needed to relieve this fucking stress.

"Mr. McCall, these are the papers that need your signature before the meeting tonight."

I heard her, but my dick is the only thing that wanted to speak back.

"Thanks Monica, can you close my door for a moment please."

Good lawd, I watched that ass sway towards the door and I was ready to put a hole in something.

"Is everything alright Mr. McCall?"

She knew damn well it wasn't, she just wanted me to say something so she could tell me how she's gonna make it better.

"I'm stressed the fuck out!"

HE THOUGHT HE HAD ME

I began taking off my suit jacket and watched her walk towards the side of my desk. She walked up to me and I laid my head on her stomach. I rubbed her legs, she parted them just enough so I could slide my index finger inside of her. This woman had some sweet tasting pussy.

She moaned slightly as she kissed the top of my head. I watched her kneel down in front of me. Watching her get on her knees, unbuckle my pants and pull out my hard dick was pure delight.

She spit on the head and started licking up and down the sides of my dick. In one swift motion she took my dick down her throat using nothing but mouth. I grabbed a hand full of her hair and kept forcing her mouth all the way down my shaft, baby was good no gagging at all.

My body tensed up, holding her head more forcefully I was ready to serve her up my hot nut. She's such a good girl, she never minds swallowing. Monica stood up and wiped her mouth, winked at me and walked back to her desk. No matter how many times she comes in here and gives me head, I never have to worry about her saying anything to anyone. I mean no woman wants to be known as the one who is only sucking a man's dick.

I showered at my office, changed into my black Armani suit and laced my body with Gucci Guilty cologne. I hope like fuck Alana ass don't be late. I don't want to have to explain the tardiness of my wife because she needed to apply lashes or some shit.

I left the office letting Monica lock up. I caught the elevator to the parking garage, jumped into my Aston Martin the Vanquish Carbon edition. One must look like making money is their motto.

I phoned Alana ass to make sure she was ready and to my surprise, she was already in the car. I saw had a missed text message from Trina when I got off the phone with Alana.

Hey baby I know we just got together but I am gonna need another dose of you as soon as possible. Call me soon.

I didn't reply back to that shit, she knows the rules and how I get down with her. She was being a typical female at this point. I just want the ones that know how to play their role, suck a mean dick, and let me fuck when I want to. All that extra shit is far from anything I want.

I walked in the restaurant, did a quick glance hoping to see Byron and or Alana, but a first glance I didn't see anyone I recognized. I stood at the door waiting for the hostess to seat me. She was pretty damn cute but she was so damn skinny, all we could do was start a fire.

I gave her my name and let her know that I was waiting for a party of two. She asked me to follow her and I was seated at a cozy table near the back. That way I could have a conversation in peace without people all in my mouth.

The hostess let me know that a waitress would be coming over shortly. I pulled my phone from my jacket to call Alana, her phone rang four times and went to voicemail. I then called Byron to see how long would be. Maybe Alana would get here before he does, but his damn phone went straight to voicemail.

The waitress came over. She was a cute chocolate dream with a nice tight ass, almond shaped dark eyes, and titties that introduced themselves first. Not to mention a tight body to hold all of that. I ran my usual rum and coke order and as she walked away, I definitely admired her backside.

In a matter of minutes, she was walking back over with my drink. I tipped her a twenty. I didn't even get my pallet wet before I looked up and saw Byron walking over with my wife. She had a drink in her hand, laughing and smiling and shit.

"Well damn, where the hell are y'all coming from? I thought everyone was running late but as I can see everyone is right on time."

I put my drink back down, and didn't take my eyes off of Alana wondering how in the fuck, she make it here before me and then not even call me to let me know. She come walking her ass over here looking like she giving the pussy away. Tight pants, fuck me pumps, breast pushed up to the heavens, and she got on more make up than I've ever seen her wear. And this nigga Byron practically got his dick in his hands.

They both spoke in unison like they have known each other forever. If Alana don't know she just fucked up, she damn sho' bout to find out tonight.

"Hey babe."

She slid inside the booth on my left side and kissed me on the cheek. I played the shit off, called her sexy sex and what not. I couldn't let this nigga stand in front of me and see me sweat. Byron sat across from us, letting me know how much good company my wife was. I wanted to lay this nigga down, the thoughts I was having about this nigga and my wife almost made me lose my cool.

"So, what you drinking sexy sex?"

She looked down at her now empty glass.

"Oh don't worry Edward, I'll have her another drink sent over. I started a tab when I walked in."

No this muthafucka didn't just offer to get my wife another drink. If she's going to be drinking, I'm going to be buying her the drinks.

"Naw man, it's cool. But thanks anyway,"

I waved down the waitress that served me my drink and grabbed two more drinks from her.

"Alright Byron, let's get down to business so me and my wife can get out of here."

I opened my briefcase, handed him all the papers signed sealed and delivered. I peeped him looking at each piece of paper intently, sighing occasionally, and seeming to not be impressed with the deal. But I knew that was bullshit, this was a 21.5 million dollar deal and I got it down to 17 million.

"Great deal Edward. How did you swing that? I mean I'm grateful. Not many houses just drop like that and not out in California, Hollywood none the less."

Byron grabbed a pen out of his suite jacket signed his name and pushed the papers back to me. I did a quick glance over the paperwork and dropped it back in my briefcase.

"Well Byron, let's just say I know quite a few people and I do a lot of business out in California, the land of the rich and famous. A happy client is a happy bank account."

I noticed Alana dropped her head when I said that, she knows I'm not lying. We all talked for about another hour or so. At that point I couldn't sit here one more minute, I was ready to bounce. Alana and I was finishing up our drinks when Byron decided to spark up one more conversation.

"Edward, your girl is funny as hell, she had me cracking up while we were waiting on you. I didn't know she could be so comical."

I see he just had to throw that last bit of information out there, as we were getting up from the table.

"Correction, my wife."

I narrowed my eyes looking at him.

"Same difference."

Alana scooted out the booth and Byron stood up to say goodbye. I stepped out the booth, gave him a firm hand shake, grabbed my wife around her waist and headed for the door.

****

I pulled into the garage, she must have gotten here minutes before I did her car was still hummin. I jumped out walked through the garage inside the house. I didn't miss a beat, I climbed the interior stairs to the bedroom two at a time. When I reached the door, Alana was sitting on the edge of the bed slipping off her shoes.

"So are you gonna speak first or should I?"

HE THOUGHT HE HAD ME

I hope she knew this was indeed not a fucking game.

"Hell you seem to have an attitude so you speak first."

I walked my ass over to the left side of the bed and took off my clothes; I knew this shit was about to go from bad to worse.

"For starters you get to the restaurant before me, then don't let me know you're there. Then you at the fucking bar with another man having drinks and what not. What kind of shit is that? Then to make matters worse, the whole fucking time we sitting at the damn table you can't seem to keep your fucking eyes off of him!"

I was ready to snap her fucking neck. It's one thing to do what the fuck you want and it's another thing to flaunt the shit.

"You sound like a fucking fool; I didn't call because I knew you were on the way. Yes I was at the bar. Good thing I seen him at your office before, otherwise I would've been looking crazy standing there looking around. And last but not least if you think I was so busy looking at someone else, then maybe you need to check the shit you do!"

I laughed out loud; I knew she would eventually go there.

HE THOUGHT HE HAD ME

I continued to take my clothes off. I walked back in front of her as she was sitting there with her head in her hands; shaking her damn head.

"I don't give two fucks what you say. You were the one all up in that man's face smiling and shit, coming from the damn bar. So don't make this shit about me. This is all about you and that nigga!"

"Oh! So now because you think someone has shown some sort of interest in me you pissed? I told your ass before you're not the only one that like this ass, so keep playing with me if you want to."

Alana stood up and was face to face with me spewing her venom of words at me. I literally saw myself choking the life out of her.

"What? Because that nigga smiled in your fucking face, you think he want your ass. Don't flatter yourself darling, he a man; all we ever want to do is FUCK!"

I stepped back from her and watched her undress and slip on her robe. I hated the words the moment they left my mouth, but looks like we hitting below the belt.

"Ain't that a bitch! If you think all he wanted to do is fuck then that's your fucking problem. If you think I want to fuck him; that is still your fucking problem. Next goddamn time don't ask me to meet you nowhere because I swear the answer is gonna be NO!"

She was giving me the ghetto girl neck roll and finger wagging the entire time she talked. I can't believe she said it's my problem. As pissed off as I was, looking at her curves under her robe my dick jumped hard and like I said to her earlier..."men only want to FUCK!"

HE THOUGHT HE HAD ME

Dana

I had just come in from work tired as hell. I walked straight to my room ready to take off everything and lay the fuck down. My phone began to ring. It wasn't late but all the people I normally talk too throughout the day, I've already spoken to. I was curious when the caller came up unknown.

"Hello."

"Hello, may I speak to Marques?"

I looked down at the phone as if it was gonna change in the palm of my hand somehow.

"Um, who the hell is this?"

"This is Shawna, his ex-wife."

I was taken back that this bitch was calling my fucking phone.

"So why the fuck are you calling my goddamn phone?"

"He gave me this number in case of an emergency and I can't get a hold of him."

This bitch has lost all her fucking mind if she think for one moment I'm gonna call him and make sure he calls her.

"Sweetheart I'm only gonna say this once and for all, don't ever call my fucking phone looking for your side dick again. How fucking lame do you have to be to call another woman's phone looking for your man. The next time you call, you'll be blocked."

I spoke in a calm manner. No sense of getting pissed off at her, hell she only doing what he told her to do.

"Whatever you say Dana. Whatever number Marques gives me, I'll call it as many times as I need to in order to speak to him."

The phone clicked off and I was furious that this nigga got the fucking nerve to be calling my fucking phone.

Tonight is the night I'm gonna hook up with the dude Marques has for me. My head already fucked up from that shit and now this shit. I just started stripping off clothes to go take a shower when I heard the fucking door chime. Marques brings his ass straight to the bedroom looking like he just jumped out of a fucking rap video.

"Hey baby, you still good for later on tonight?"

I didn't say shit to him. I kept right on gathering my things for my shower. He kept right on talking while scrolling through his phone, never really looking up at me.

HE THOUGHT HE HAD ME

"Well Dee, the hotel is nice. It's Downtown so you'll be in good hands. You won't have any problems."

I stopped in my tracks, turned and watched him as he ran his mouth about nothing that I cared to hear about.

"Damn Marques, I just walked in the house. As you can see my naked body standing here on my way to take a shower. I don't want to hear shit about tonight until I come out the fucking bathroom!"

I left him standing right in the fucking doorway playing with his phone. I heard him mumble some shit as I was closing the door.

I made sure I stayed my ass in the shower for an hour. I honestly thought to myself about all this bullshit this man want me to do and that I agreed to. This can't be love.

When I walked out the bathroom I had a white plush bath towel wrapped around my body and to my surprise Marques ass was still in the fucking room sitting on the edge of the bed watching sports on T.V.

Marques got up and approached me, grabbing me around my waist, planting kisses on my neck like we were some happy ass couple.

"Dana you know you got some good ass pussy. This shit is gonna be in and out and I won't be far from you."

HE THOUGHT HE HAD ME

I just wanted to spit on the mere thought of him even wanting me to do some shit like this. This lets me know its Marques bus and I'm just a passenger. I was almost in tears here. I have a man that at the very touch of his hands makes my pussy thump and then at the very sound of his voice can piss me off.

"What's with the tears Dana? Tonight isn't the night for this shit. I hope you're not trying to back out of this? Look baby I want you to just relax yourself, take a shot or two and pretend that you are with me; even if you have to instruct that nigga to fuck you the way that I do."

Marques put his arms around me holding me tight like this shit was going to make it all better. At this very moment, I went into game mode. I shook off the butterflies and went and got ready for my night.

I wore a black lace thong and bra set, draped a body hugging black dress over my body that showed every curve I had. My hair, make-up was on point, I slipped my stilettos on and checked myself in the mirror. Turned and looked at Marques.

"Well what do you think?"

I did a quick spin so he could see what ol' boy was about to get.

"Damn Dee, you look like you bout' to fuck the shit out of him."

"That is the plan...right?"

"Yeah it's the plan alright."

As we walked out the room before we reached the door, I looked at him cause' I wasn't about to let this shit just pass me by.

"As long as you fucking live and I'm doing shit like this for you, don't you ever have another bitch call my fucking phone looking for you!"

I didn't want to hear no fucking excuses. I just was ready to get this night over with. When we got in the car Marques reached over and kissed me.

"I'll handle that shit Dee."

****

Headed to the hotel I was having all sorts of mixed emotions. Every time I looked over at Marques I couldn't believe this shit was actually going to happen. Hell I guess I should be thankful that his ass didn't want me to work the street.

The street hoes and then he has what he calls tops hoes and that's his real big money. We pulled up to the hotel, we parked as we walked into the hotel. He put his hand on the small of my back, I don't know what kind of picture he's trying to paint but it is frameless.

Got the room number where I'm going to be entertaining. He kissed me on my lips and walked out. I got five hours to get this shit done and over with. I walked to the elevators, I turned to look at him and he was already heading out the door and didn't even look back.

I hopped my ass on the elevator and pushed the number forty-four. At this point I was ready to get in and get out. I walked to the door that had forty-four on it, two knocks was all it took for him to open the door.

When the door opened, there he stood 6'3 and fine as fuck! He gestured for me to come in, I walked my ass in that room swaying my ass just a little harder. Whatever issues I had before I got to this room, I can safely say there long gone now.

He immediately introduced his self and I was pleased to meet Terry. We made the normal small talk introductions. I sat at the bar while he fixed both of us a drink. I gulped my first on in a matter of minutes, all he did was smile and fixed me another one.

"So Terry, is this some normal type of shit you do or is this a one-time thing? I mean you're a very handsome guy, you could practically have any woman you want. So why pay for sex?"

HE THOUGHT HE HAD ME

Once I start drinking it don't take much to get my lips to moving. He has a fit body from what I can tell, low hair cut and goatee; this man was simply handsome to me. He put his glass down before he spoke.

"I got tired of women trying to play this mind game with me, thinking that just because I do have the finer things in life that's an open door for them to walk through and expect me to take care of them. But don't get me wrong, if she my woman she gets it all. But when I see she has dollar signs in her eyes, she got it wrong and got me fucked up."

Listening to him I found out that he is into stocks, sounds kind of geeky for my taste but hell it makes him a lot of money. I noticed he poured the last two shots of Black Hennessey in our glasses. I stood up from the bar I reached my hand out to him…play time was over.

We walked to the bedroom, I was ready for anything at this moment. It was time some fucking went on in here. I turned to face him, he leaned in closer and inhaled my scent as I inhaled his. I grabbed him around his neck and brought him down on the bed with me. I accepted his tongue, his touch on the side of my body was tantalizing, his grip was firm and I felt his knees part my legs so he could feel the softness and wetness of my pussy.

I was almost amazed at how wet I was becoming. Soft kisses were planted all over my neck leading to my breast, where each breast was pulled from my dress and nipples sucked immediately. I felt the bulge growing and at moment I lost it.

"Fuck me Terry!"

I wasn't about to keep playing with all this foreplay. I wanted to be dicked down now.

At that moment he stood up and undressed, I pulled my dress up over my damn head. His dick stood at attention, my pussy was inviting him in. He slipped my panties off and in one swift motion he eased his dick in me. I felt like calgon was taking me away at that very moment.

My legs were pushed back to my ears and he pounded like no man has ever pounded in my pussy before. The sound of skin slapping was heard, mixed with deep moans. He continued to pound harder and harder. I knew he was about to nut. He pulled out, I sat up and let him lay his nut on my lips.

He trailed his tongue down to my awaiting pussy and ate me from my clit to my asshole, making my pussy jump over and over again. I couldn't hold my cum any longer, I gave his face a creamy bath.

We were breathing heavy. The room felt like it was spinning, he collapsed next to me and we laid there looking up at the ceiling for a while. Two hours had passed and it was shower time for me, I got dressed and was ready to say my goodbyes.

HE THOUGHT HE HAD ME

As I walked to the door, he walked behind me. I felt his eyes admiring my ass.

"Marques said you would be well worth it. I just wish you were mine and mine only."

That shit took me back, I was not only stunned but now confused.

"Um, why the hell would you say something like that?"

"Anytime a woman would go to extreme lengths to make her man happy and he still doesn't know how to fucking treat her, then yes, I see an opportunity to come for you and make you mines. I have known Marque's ass for a while and he is and always have been bad news. He just so happen to have what I wanted and needed. I just didn't know it was going to come in such a beautiful package."

I was smiling hard on the inside. A man standing in front of me just paid to have sex with me, now he wants to be my man. This shit can't be real, but if it is, I might just see where the fuck this goes. In the meantime, I have to cut this conversation short.

"I'm flattered beyond measure...I truly am, but I don't see how any of this will work. But thank you for making me feel better than I ever have sexually and mentally."

HE THOUGHT HE HAD ME

I had no choice but to walk away, I couldn't even let him get another word in as we hugged. He kissed me with so much passion I could have passed out, but all I did was left.

Approaching the double doors in the lobby, I was greeted by Marques sitting in his black Impala waiting on me.

Now some shit just don't make any damn sense. These men really think they're the fucking KANGs around here. I hope these women understand the position they hold because they have always had the power.

HE THOUGHT HE HAD ME

Alana

I walked through the hospital with my clip-board ready to put in a full day of work when I hear my name being yelled over and over again. I didn't even have to look, I already knew whose big mouth it was. I stopped in my tracks and turned to see Terrell speed walking towards me.

"Ms. Thang! I see you taking three months off! Is everything alright?" Terrell asked, popping his lips and exaggerating every word.

I really wasn't in the mood to deal with him at this point.

"Good Morning to you too Terrell. There'll be a staff meeting this afternoon and I'll discuss everything at that time."

I began to walk away when Terrell cleared his throat, not satisfied with what I just said.

"Ms. Thang please don't try and treat me like the rest of these folks up in here. We good, so start talking please and thank you."

No matter what I say he wasn't about to let this go.

"Well since you must know now, I have some issues at home that I need to escape from, and I need a vacation."

HE THOUGHT HE HAD ME

My statement seem to have been satisfactory for Terrell, he nodded his head and told me he understood. I was glad that was the end of it, sometimes he doesn't know when to leave well enough alone.

I looked down at my clip-board and saw that a woman was here to a pregnancy test done. I asked Terrell to give her one and I would be in shortly afterwards to give her the results.

I went to the room, sat on the stainless steel stool while the patient sat on the table. I glanced over my paper work.

"Well Ms. Gibson,"

She cut me off before I could say another word.

"Please call me Shawna."

"Okay Shawna, you're definitely pregnant. According to the information that you provided your due date is April 2nd."

I like telling patients good news but this was anything from good news to her.

Now I'm no dummy, I knew who this chick was the first moment I walked in the damn room. Out of all hospitals, why in the hell would she come here, and I fuck around and have to be the one to tell her the news, and there is no doubt in my mind that punk ass Marques is the father.

HE THOUGHT HE HAD ME

This is so fucked up on so many levels. I gave Shawna her instructions on what do to throughout her pregnancy. She left the room, and with a big ass smile on her face might I add.

I tried my damnest to get through all my patients in record time today. I wasn't about to stay around this fucking place no longer than I had to. When I looked up, I was gathering my shit to leave and wasn't looking back.

I was headed to Edward's office to see if we could grab a bite, try and spend a little time before I went on my trip. I get my ass to his office he informs me that he going out of town his damn self. Now I do know whenever he just pops up and goes out of town, it always has to do with some other woman. This game of his has gone on long enough and at this point it is just plan ol' tired.

****

This muthafucka didn't even come home first before he left for his trip. I guess he had his shit at the office already. This dude is really going to the extreme of wanting to do what the fuck he wants to do.

I finally decided to turn the television off. I couldn't sleep anyway, I knew it was only because I've been deciding on whether or not to tell Dana that Shawna is pregnant, and whether to confront Edward about him fucking around.

Either way, this shit is keeping me up at night. Just the other day I received a package in the mail. When I opened it, it was credit card statements noting the places that Edward has gone when he's on his trips. I was amazed when a note came attached to it saying. *"It's time you knew the truth."*

I didn't doubt for one second that it was from Monica, his secretary. Which only lets me know that he must didn't do something she wanted him to do, and so to get back at him she decides to think she's letting me in on his secret affairs.

I was in another head space, as I looked up at the ceiling. The only light that was illuminating was from the clock on the night stand. I was wide awake and my husband was off fucking someone. In that minute, I sprang from the bed, grabbed my purse, and searched for my phone. I scrolled through my texts and got to the one that made me smile.

In record time, I was dressed in an all black cat suit that draped low around the breast and slid my feet into my highest of stilettos. I grabbed my keys and out the door I went. Yeah it was almost 11 at night but so what, I was going to take a chance.

As usual this place had a full parking lot. Many people were coming and going. I walked in and made a bee line straight towards the bar. I sat my purse in my lap, ordered me a Patron' with sprite, and made small talk to the different men that were coming up to me and introducing themselves. I was not interested but it doesn't cost to be nice.

I was on my second glass of Patron' when I heard a familiar voice behind me. I wanted to turn around but I knew I didn't want him to see how ecstatic I was to see him.

"Well, well, well. What brings a shining star out so late and none the less, by herself?"

I turned slightly in my chair to face him and no matter what I couldn't conceal my smile.

"Honestly I was hoping I would run into you."

I couldn't believe I just said that shit. Damn he must think I'm some sort of stalker and shit.

"I love your honesty. More women should do it more often."

I was practically acting like a high school girl that was finally having lunch with her crush. But Byron was definitely bringing out some feelings.

"Would you like to join me in a drink?"

I was on my second, I didn't need a third but if he said yes, then dammit I'll be drinking.

HE THOUGHT HE HAD ME

"Actually I have reached my limit because I'm driving but I can sit here with you and continue talking."

He spoke in a tone that was firm yet sincere. If he thinks all I wanted to do was talk, he is crazy as hell. I gulped down my drink. It was time we left; I came to do what I needed to do.

"In that case we should be getting out of here then."

I gave my most seductive look, when he walked up closer to me and lightly traced the outline of the left side of my face.

I grabbed my purse, he put his hand on the small of my back and we left the restaurant. His car was two lanes behind me. I pulled out and he followed. I looked out my rearview and smiled. I knew he was going to be just what I needed.

Upon reaching my home, we both parked in the garage. Once inside I could've offered him a drink, cut on some music, but we just did all of that. I told him he could follow me into my bedroom. He didn't miss a beat because when I turned and looked at him, he was right behind me smiling.

I couldn't have been in the room for more than ten seconds when he grabbed me and stuck his tongue down my throat. My mouth accepted him and my body accepted him. During our tongue wrestle, we were stepping out of our clothes, and in one swift motion, he scooped me up holding me right under my ass. I felt like I was about to faint the fact that someone has picked me up was unheard of.

"Wait baby! Please put me down. You know damn well I'm too fucking heavy for you to be trying to show out."

Whether he was showing out or not, I was fucking amazed. This type of shit Edward would never try and attempt.

"Don't worry baby, I got you. See...I got you."

Lawd, this man was fine and fit. Hell anyone that can pick me up and not tremble was right up my alley. Shit I feel like I'm on a celestial rollercoaster. Something about the way he said I got you, tells me it was much more than our position we were holding right at this moment.

He leaned me up against the wall closest to us, my legs wrapped around his waist, his tongue traveling over my neck, shoulders, and lips. Repeatedly this man was making me feel so good in a short time that I was shocked. I knew he wanted me when we first met at the restaurant but because I'm married, unhappily married. I was going to have to make the first move.

He knew the first night that he wasn't in this alone. Especially after I found that he and Edward were only associates, I started putting a game plan together and two weeks later here we are.

I felt him grow under the heat of my moist pussy. We locked eyes briefly which was a pure indication of, 'I know we don't have condoms but go ahead anyway.'

He slid inside me and I gasped for air. With every inch I felt like I was being stretched to the max. I held him around his neck, our kissing was intense and electrifying.

When he was all in, he pounded inside me and caught a rhythm that let him dance inside my walls. I couldn't turn this man away even if I wanted to. I just knew at this very moment I was loving the pain he was giving me.

HE THOUGHT HE HAD ME

Marques

It's been damn near a week since she got with ol' boy and if she think I'm gonna keep going days without saying a word about what took place, she crazy as hell. I'm trying to be a little understanding but I couldn't keep waiting on her to get up the nerve and talk to me about her fucking another man.

This man paid twenty grand to fuck and I want to know how well he fucked her. The clients that pay that kind of money are generally men, coming from out of town. They don't want nothing but sex and maybe a night out on the town. They damn sure didn't want no crazy ass bitch following him and his money once he left his kids drying on her face.

I caught Dana coming out the bathroom dressed like she was ready to start her day.

"Well damn baby, you up and dressed and you still haven't said anything about what happened with you and ol' boy."

I don't know why she was making this shit so damn difficult.

"Look Marques, you asked for a favor that required me to fuck and be fucked as long as he wanted to in the course of a few hours. There is nothing to talk about unless you want to know how he ate my pussy, or how I sucked his dick, or how he fucked me do damn good all I could do was cry out in pure ecstasy. But of course you don't want to hear no shit like that now do you?"

I was so fucking ready to knock her fucking teeth out. How dare she talk to me like I'm some punk ass on the fucking street? The images that she has painted in my fucking head in all honesty is fucking me up; which is pissing me off by the second.

"Oh I see we got a smart ass mouth this morning. Well Dee, enlighten me; did he fuck you good? How did he eat your pussy? And for the sake of saying, how well did you suck his dick? I mean after all, you did have a job to do."

If this bitch thought she was about to get one up on me like she was gonna tear me down with that shit, she messing with the wrong muthafucker.

"Well like you said boo, I had a job to do and let's just say it was a job well done. It won't surprise me if he calls and want to request me again. But we both know that was a onetime deal...right?"

I watched her as she left the room with her belongings. I know one damn thing, I was done with this conversation. I wasn't gonna ask her anything else as long as I got my money, I hoped she swallowed his babies.

My fucking phone kept going off like every ten minutes. It was a text message from Shawna saying, "to call her ASAP!" I didn't want to hear shit she had to say. I really didn't, but if I didn't go see what the fuck she had to say, she wouldn't let up on me.

I was already dressed, I left and went to see Shawna. I hope like hell she wasn't on no bullshit this morning. I jumped in my Impala and headed her way. I threw some old school Tupac on and cruised the city until I got to her house.

I ran straight up in the house seeing that I have a key and all. I wasn't the knocking on the door kind of nigga. If we fucking I better have access to her fucking house, it's those other niggas that have to knock. I walked in yelling Shawna name not seeing her anywhere, I went to the kitchen to grab a cold beer.

"Why the hell are you yelling my fucking name? I was right here in the bedroom. All you had to do was walk upstairs and find me."

I wasn't in the mood to play come find the hoe.

"First off, why the hell do you have it so damn hot in here? It's the middle of October and you got this fucking place feeling like Florida up in this muthafucka."

Damn when she walked her ass in the kitchen, I didn't know whether to talk to her or fuck her.

"Nigga please, this my house. You live with little miss Dana, so don't worry about what I keep the heat on up in here,"

She has got to be killing me. She must have memory loss on who the fuck pay these bills around this bitch.

"You must have forgot who the hell pay your bills. So all that lip, you can miss me with it."

I sat down at the kitchen table looking at her, wishing she would say another fucking word. I wasn't on this shit with her today.

"Hell, so I'm here. What the hell is so damn important that you blowing up my damn phone?"

Shawna walked over and grabbed a seat looking like she just won the lottery.

"Do you remember July 4th?"

I couldn't even answer because as she talked, she smiled a thousand smiles.

"Um, yes but what the hell that got to do with right now?"

The look of confusion was painted on my face, I didn't know where she was going with this.

"Well, because you invited me to Vic's 4th of July party, we ended up fucking in the one of his many bedrooms. So long story short…I'm pregnant."

This shit just hit me like a ton of bricks, there's no way she's pregnant. I mean yeah, we always fuck without condoms but I always pull out…well at least most of the time anyway.

"Damn Shawna! Are you one hundred percent sure? I swear I aint ready for no damn kids."

Fuck! This shit has just fucked my whole understanding. And she got the nerve to be smiling like this is something that either one of us need right now. Fuck! Dana gonna kill my ass about this shit.

Shawna grabbed my hand and asked me to follow her, I was apprehensive about it but I did. We went into the bedroom that I haven't been in for seven years. The walls had out wedding picture on it and the sonogram of our twins that she miscarried was on the wall as well.

"Damn girl, you still got out wedding picture on the wall and the twins. I can't believe you haven't change this room not one bit."

This shit was kind of bitter sweet and I was ready to leave; I'm not trying to relive the past. She walked through the room touching every piece of baby furniture and pulling out old baby clothes. I understood what she was trying to do which further lets me know, she had all the plans in the world to keep this baby.

"Yeah I didn't want to throw anything away. I knew I would use this room again, I just didn't know when. But I must say that I feel like god is giving us another chance at having a real family, as long as you don't but your hands on me again and cause me to have another miscarriage.

"I apologized for that seven years ago. Had you not punched me in the face during an argument, I wouldn't have slapped the shit out of you, causing you to lose your balance and fall down the stairs."

If she think I'm about to sit here and go down memory lane about this, she crazy as fuck. But I do have one question for her ass though. I need to know who baby is that anyway mines or Vic's.

****

Leaving Shawna house I knew at some point she was gonna been bothering me about wanting to lay down some music to some banging ass tracks, but we ain't gonna do none of that until I see if he got Shawna pregnant or is it really mines.

I couldn't make it to the studio good before my damn phone started ringing off the damn hook. I looked at the number wondering what the fuck Tay was doing calling me. She knows to only call this number in a serious emergency.

"What up Tay?"

"Marques you have to get to the hospital quick it's Rochelle."

I made a u-turn and headed to the County Hospital.

"What happened to her?"

"All I know she was laying in an alley when I was about to do a job, she really messed up. I almost didn't recognize her."

I'm on the way see you in about twenty minutes."

I hung up the phone and made my way to the hospital.

I walked through the doors of the hospital and asked for directions to where my sister was at. When I saw her face with all the dried up tears that has stained her face, I knew it wasn't going to be good.

"Marques! I'm so damn glad you finally got here."

"What room she in Tay?"

"302, they say she brain dead Marques,"

Tay looked at me like she wanted me to wave my magic wand and make it all go away.

"I can't fix this one baby girl," I softly spoke in her ear and kissed her forehead.

We both walked into the room and seeing Rochelle hooked up to more tubes than I can count was ridiculous. I walked over to the bed while Tay hung to my arm for dear life. I hung my head low until I heard the door swing open. A short fat guy walked in with a clipboard.

"I'm Dr. Roth and I'm gonna be straight up with the both of you. Rochelle has lost all brain movement, she has shattered facial bones, and we had to remove a broken bottle from her vagina. So from this point on I need to know what actions you would like to take seeing that she put you down assuming your name is Marques as next of kin."

I was thrown back by what the Doc was telling me but I had to make this shit as painless as possible.

"I want her taken off the machines now."

Tay jerked away from me with tear filled eyes.

"What the hell you mean take her off Marques?"

"Look Tay, the damn doctor said she is brain dead. There ain't shit we can do and unless you have heard of a brain dead muthafucka selling pussy, then this is the only way I see!"

Tay didn't break eye contact with me at all.

"You know what Marques, I've always known you to be a cold ass bastard. I just hope hell is the best place for you to be. Do what the fuck you want I'm out of here."

Once Tay left the damn room, I looked at the doctor without even blinking.

"Cut the machines off and cremate her today!"

I walked out of the room and didn't turn back.

HE THOUGHT HE HAD ME

Dana

I can't believe how good Terry was; fuck! That man can serve me the dick anytime he wishes. I knew I had to call my girl, I haven't spoken to her in what seems like weeks. I got some shit to tell her. The phone rang twice before she answered.

"WHERE THE FUCK HAVE YOU BEEN?"

I couldn't do nothing but laugh because I knew she was thinking the same damn thing I'm thinking.

"Don't even try it! Where the hell have you been Ms. Thang?"

"Gurl I got some shit to tell you."

Alana was very theatrical whenever she spoke and she knew she had some juicy shit to tell me.

"Wait before you go deep on me. Why aren't you at work?"

"Gurl, I took three months off, I needed a fucking break. That job gonna be right there when I get the fuck back. Hell, I rarely take days off and since we get roll over days, I'm taking me a nice long vacation."

"That's good to hear because I'm going home for Thanksgiving and you should come with me. It'll be like when we were kids."

"Sounds like I plan, I'm on board. So now that that's out the way, let me tell you about this guy I met."

I couldn't believe my damn ears. Did she just say some man she just met? Not the way she all in love with Edward. I didn't see this shit coming.

"He is an associate Of Edwards; I went to a meeting with him and Edward was late, so let's just say Byron and I hit it off real well. And now that he has felt the inside of my flesh I'm floating on cloud nine."

Did I just hear this shit right? She out here fucking other dudes while her man, wait her husband is on a business trip. I couldn't do anything but smile the whole damn time she was speaking; I knew that shit was going to happen eventually.

She went on to tell me that she wasn't expecting nothing much, but when she went back to the restaurant looking for him, she knew she was ready to venture from under her cheating ass husband. All I can say is kudos to her.

"Damn chick you've been busy but I like your style. Hell I don't know how mines gonna top that."

I was on pin and needles to tell her about Terry.

"Well this new guy I'm seeing and very much interested in, I think he gonna be the one I leave Marques ass for."

"Oh shit! Did you say leave Marques?"

"Yes you heard right, we both know he ain't no damn good and that shit has ran its course. So Marques had a proposition for me. I was furious at the shit he asked me to do but that's how I met Terry and he is a great guy. "

"So let me get this right, Marques asked you to hook up with some dude. You do so and now you are seeing him? Damn I guess that pipe was laid right like a muthafucka!"

After she said that we both laughed loud as hell, but she was right. Even though I don't see it as pay back, I know when and if Marques finds out that I'm letting Terry dick me down, he might think about how the fuck he treats the next chick.

We continued to talk about the possible new men in our lives and just how we want happiness just like any other woman. The only thing was, we knew we were not going to have that with the men that we were currently with.

I walked around my photo studio making sure all inventory was in place, and making sure I've booked my last shoot before I go out of town. Still listening to Alana talk about this Byron dude, from what she says he seems to be good for her; but as we both know only time will tell.

My phone buzzed. I had a text message, I was going to check it later but figured it might be important.

A week has been long enough good thing I already had your number, now you have mines. Terry

"Um Alana boo, I don't mean to cut you off but um I do have to call you back. The phone clicked off and I sat down in my plush leather chair and reread the text. I was smiling from ear to ear. Now I'm wondering what took him so long to contact me. When I left the room I did give him my number and told him to call when he was ready. Had I had his number I would've been called, but I damn sure was about to text him back.

Well, well, well it is about time you contacted me it is such a welcome.

In a few seconds my phone buzzed again.

I was trying to make sure this is what we both want

I felt like a damn high school girl with a crush and was floating on cloud nine because he was texting me.

It is what we want. I want another dose of what you gave me before...lol

Let's make a date for it and I'll be willing to dick you down again.

Can you say Marques who? Shit we gonna make us a date; I got to have that dick again and again.

No problem, next time I will call you and let you know where to meet me at.

I'll wait on it.

All I could do was shake my head and smile thinking the way we met was very unconventional but dammit it seems to be working for us. If I can deal with Marques ass, I damn sure can deal with Terry.

My phone began to ring and to my surprise it's my girl Alana.

"Hey Chick."

"Hey, I'm calling back because I had something to tell you that's kind of important."

Oh shit I hope her husband haven't found out about Byron ass, it wouldn't surprise me one bit if he had some damn PI following her.

"Okay I am listening."

"I was at work and in my office sat Shawna, Marques ex-wife and I had to tell her that she was pregnant. We didn't discuss who the daddy was but I'm sure we both know."

I think my ears stopped listening after the words Shawna and pregnant.

"How far along is she?"

"She is three months and her due date is in July. This goes against everything in my profession but I had to let you know."

"I really appreciate you telling me. I really do but it was bound to happen, this is just a wake-up call for me to get my shit together and move on. As you know it's been a hard road with him and enough is enough."

I was shocked that he would even get someone else pregnant but that was the typical Marques, he only cares about him and everyone and everything is second.

Once we got off the phone I knew it was something I had to do. I didn't give two fucks if I was at home in the bed and Marques ass walked around butt ass naked; playtime was over.

Meet me at the Embassy tomorrow at 7p.m. room 620.

I knew this was wrong to immediately call his ass after Alana tells me some other bitch is carrying his baby but dammit I won't allow myself to cry over it. A few seconds later my phone buzzed.

Will be there.

HE THOUGHT HE HAD ME

****

The moment had finally come for Terry and I to finally get together again, when a woman is fed the fuck up with dealing with bullshit she will make the necessary changes to her life and that's exactly what the hell I am doing; making the necessary changes to my life.

I never thought that I would've come to a moment like this in my life that I would be able to finally get my head right and leave Marques alone. But in life, we never know what paths we're gonna travel. Some we can control and some we cannot, and my life I can control.

I watched Marques lay his clothes on the bed as I was walking through the bedroom door with a bag of new lingerie for tonight. He was smelling all good and looking all good. He had on his black boxer briefs and his black wife beater. His chocolate smooth skin was damn near illuminating. I shook my head while I walked over to the closet and sat my bag down.

"Are you on your way out?"

I didn't have to ask but I did to save face. He stopped rubbing his body oil into his skin and looked at me.

HE THOUGHT HE HAD ME

"Yes I am why do you ask?"

"No real reason other than I just wanted to know."

This man was looking so damn good to me if I wasn't tired of his shit, I would probably fuck the shit out of him right now.

Marques met me at the closet and held my hands, looked me deep in the eye and without even breaking a sweat he went on ahead and told me.

"Look Dana, there is no easy way for me to say this so I'm gonna just be straight up with you. I found out that Shawna is pregnant, she's keeping it and I'm not about to hide my seed from you and nobody else. All I can say I hope you don't leave me but if you do, it's nothing that I can do about it."

Thank goodness Alana already gave me the heads up so now the ball was in my court. I let his hands go and I watched him return to getting his self ready.

Before he put his jeans on I walked slowly to him, chest to chest, mouth to mouth and kissed his as passionately as I could remember I did the very first time we made love.

He fell into my kiss, his hands found their way to the back of my head, he pressed our mouths tighter together. I broke our kiss my trailing my tongue over his chin, across his neck, down the middle of his chest stopping to tease each nipple, making my way down to his awaiting dick.

I slid his boxer briefs off and let the head of his dick dance on my lips before I let my tongue taste him. I slowly let him slide his dick into my mouth until I felt the head of his dick touch my throat. My rhythm was slow and steady until I picked up the pace. I felt his hands entangled in my hair that's when he began to fuck my mouth. Slurping sounds were being made, I looked up at him as he pounded my mouth over and over making me gag every time. I felt his body tense up and before I knew it he sprayed my mouth with his cum. I let that shit ooze out of my mouth. His body starting calming down as he sat on the bed and looked at me with confusion.

I went to the adjoining bathroom brushed my teeth and rinsed my mouth out, walked back in as he was putting on a pair of dark denim Levis, grabbed him on the side of his face and kissed him one last time.

"I hope you have a great night."

I wasn't mad. I knew I needed and deserved better, and I knew he wasn't about to change and I was done trying to make him change.

When he left it was time. I grabbed my shit and got ready for Terry tonight. Time was flying the entire day I got ready to make myself look beautiful for him. I knew he was ready just from the text saying he couldn't wait to see me. I felt like my life was on a new path and I was ready to enjoy it. I wasn't gonna let the New Year come and go with the same bullshit!

I love the sistahs especially when they start making great choices about who they gonna give their heart and that monkey to. Let's see if they keep their smarts, so far so good.

Its holiday time!

HE THOUGHT HE HAD ME

Edward
Thanks Giving

Here I am sitting in this lavish hotel room with a bitch who I'm sick and tired of. I don't love her at this point. She's just habit, a fucking habit that I need to break.

I been fucking her one day too damn long. It's time I get back to what the fuck matters and that's my damn wife who is probably sitting at home missing me, and that's where the hell I should be. Slicing hot turkey with her instead I am sitting on this king size bed at my favorite spot in Miami letting this bitch Trina suck my dick.

Usually I would be trying to ram my damn dick down her throat but right now all I want is for her to finish.

I left home yesterday on my usual business trip. Alana seemed to be cool with it, she didn't mention anything about it being the holidays and how she wanted me to stay home. She hugged me and let me walk out the door. Guess she fed up with this shit too.

I looked down at the top of Trina head and pushed her away she been sucking my dick for all of twenty minutes and I'm not fully hard, that shit don't happen to a well endowed brotha like myself. Trina kept being persistent trying to grab the head with her lips or jag me off. I simply didn't want any of this shit anymore.

"Damn baby what's up? You acting like you don't want my head game this morning."

I couldn't do nothing and look perplexed. There were no words that I could say that wouldn't hurt her feelings. So I just stood up walked to the bar and fixed me a drink.

"You know Trina, we have been dealing for a while now and sweetie, I think our time has run its course. I mean you're a beautiful woman but I do have commitments that I have been neglecting for some time now. For goodness sake, look where we're on Thanksgiving."

Trina didn't move she just sat there on the floor nodding her head. I just wasn't sure if she was agreeing with me or was it the silence before the storm.

"You are right Edward, this doesn't feel right and anytime I put your dick in my mouth and you don't get off we have definitely come to an end. I always knew what this was, sex and nothing but sex and I was cool with that but just like you already have, I want someone to come home to as well."

I was shocked that she felt that way. I just knew she was going to start ranting and raving about why we can't be together and all that shit.

I was not about to dig deeper into this shit. I just knew I was ready to go. In order not to have a fight with her while I'm trying to put my house back together, I offered to send her away with a six figure severance package.

She wasn't always about the money. I knew she had very strong feeling for me, she said she loved me; just wasn't quite sure.

She decided to go home for the holidays as well. We packed our shit up and headed for the very next flights going in separate directions.

One last thing I had to do before I boarded the plane.

Sexy sex I am coming home.

Then I pushed send.

HE THOUGHT HE HAD ME

Alana

I was so excited when we finally landed at the Atlanta Airport this morning, I didn't know what to do. Dana went straight to her mom who is cool; it gave me a chance to have phone sex with Byron twice before showering and relaxing some.

This man in the last six weeks has made me feel better than Edward has made me feel in six years. When I knew he started cheating, I over looked it, but I continued to play the doting wife to keep my home as normal as possible.

I knew that shit was coming to an end. I just didn't know it would be with a man who loves and adores me and to be someone that Edward knows; I guess life is funny that way.

I didn't even call Edward when I got here, something I usually do when he's out of town. Since I was going out of town my damn self, I figure I'll let him figure this one out on his own. He's a pretty smart man and when he left I didn't give any of the old shit I use to do, like begging him to stay or take me with him.

Those days are long over and I will not repeat that shit. All I wanted to do at this point was get divorced, eat some good food, see family I haven't seen in years and plan a great future with Byron.

I literally gave Edward the best of me and he didn't appreciate it. It was a marriage learned. I can't believe he had the nerve to send me a text talking about he's on his way back home.

I couldn't do nothing but laugh at that knowing that he would be there by his damn self. Hell, he was my main reason for taking so much time off, but now that I have all my ducks lined up in a row I don't need it now.

I was relaxed lying across this big pretty ass bed when my damn phone broke my concentration. I looked down at it and I should have known it was Dana ass.

"Hey chick."

"Don't hey chick me. We've been here for two hours all ready and you ain't here yet. You need me to come pick you up, what's taking you so damn long?"

Guess I won't get any rest today.

"No. You don't have to come get me. I'll be there in an hour and by the way, it's only 11 o'clock. I know the food isn't ready yet or is it?"

"Look girl, you know my momma don't play most of the food was ready yesterday, so get your ass here...bye."

No matter what, this woman wasn't gonna let me rest. It's cool though, I was ready to grub and mingle. I hopped up, got dressed, checked myself in the mirror and was out the door. The hotel had taxis lined up I jumped in one and was headed to Dana's mommas house.

As I sat in the back seat of the taxi, I started to reminisce about how Dana, her sister and I would run the streets hard. Dana and her sister are only two years apart so she was old enough to hang with us. Hell I haven't seen Trina ass in years, I wonder how the hell she was doing?

HE THOUGHT HE HAD ME

Marques

"Happy Turkey day baby!"

Is this girl serious? I could care less about a damn Turkey day. It's just like any other day as far as I am concerned.

"Damn girl, I don't give a shit about no damn holiday! If it doesn't involve me getting money then I don't care about it."

I couldn't get that shit Dana did when I told her that Shawna was pregnant out of my head.

She has always given me outstanding head but damn it that shit was like she was sucking my soul out with it. I can't lie this shit kind of fucking with my head. I didn't want to argue with her so I've been laying low with Shawna. I thought it was best we had a little time apart but the killing thing is I haven't heard shit from her, no text, no call, no nothing. Guess she more pissed off than I thought.

I had to go see my man Vic. He said he needed to holla at me about something. I hope like hell it isn't about this damn music thing again because I may just have to cuss him out. I'm really tired of hearing about it.

Shawna pressing me about coming with her to her momma house. That shit is not about to happen. After I take my ass by Vic's studio, I'll be taking my ass home. Dana shouldn't be home by herself on a holiday. Even though I don't care about it, I do have love for her.

Shawna pierced my ears by whining about me not staying with her today clean up until I started up my damn truck. I let Tupac mellow me the fuck out while I drove the Chicago city streets.

Finally hitting the studio I saw his truck already out back. I made the usual call so he could have the door unlocked for me. I walked and ran into a thick cloud of smoke, just what I need to get the day started. Slapping hands with the fellas as they offered me some mean green.

"What up Vic man?"

I slapped hands with him and sat in one of the black leather studio chairs while he played around with different beats so we could hear it.

"Damn my nigga, where the fuck you been? I haven't seen nor heard from your ass."

He talking and smoking at the same damn time. That smoke must've went down the wrong damn pipe cause my nigga started coughing hard as hell. A person who don't know nothing about smoking would have thought that he was about pass out, but the rest of us knew he was about to be extremely high in about 2.5 seconds.

"Man my nigga, I been around trying to dodge the drama out here with these women and shit. Other than that, my shit on point as usual."

I took another toke of the mean green. Vic looked at me with a smirk, I didn't quite know what the fuck his problem was but I don't take kind to niggas smiling all at me and shit.

"I need to holla at you in the back for a minute if you don't mind."

I rose up from the chair not knowing what the hell he could've been ready talk to me about, especially something so important that he didn't want to say in front of the fellas.

We walked to the back room where he stored extra equipment and mics. The room was poorly lit, I stood in the door way while he sat on a small table that was covered with CD's

"Alright my nigga, what's this about?"

"I wanted you to hear it from me cause we go way back and I don't want you to think I'm bullshitting you in no kinda way."

"Aye my nigga I take my liquor straight."

Everyone knew what that meant. I said, that meaning 'stop beating around the bush'.

"I been fucking Shawna for a minute and...

I cut that nigga off so he couldn't say shit else. Now I was pissed.

"Is this about some bitch?"

"Look man that's your ex- wife and shit. She told me she was pregnant so I wanted you to know she said she was gonna tell you, but as a man I thought I needed to say something."

I can't believe this nigga brought some bitch shit to me. I could care less who the fuck him or her is fucking. This shit is crazy as hell!

"My nigga let me explain something so we don't ever have this kinda conversation again. A bitch is a bitch to me, nothing more nothing less. If she letting you fuck, don't stop on my account; hell I got a woman. Trust me man its all good, but like I say hoes do hoe shit so please don't trip. We cool my nigga. But let me ask you something. Who baby is she carrying mines or yours?"

I'm not gonna take care of another niggas seed fuck that.

"It's yours my nigga, we always use condoms. But I'm about to go on tour so I won't be around anyway."

We laughed that shit off. If it's one thing I don't worry about, it's what a bitch is doing. I've been on these streets long enough to know that bitches are subject to do anything and act like they're innocent; cussing you the fuck out for fucking her home girl. Yeah time for me to make amends with Dana, because Shawna ass is as old as yesterday's news paper.

HE THOUGHT HE HAD ME

Dana

"Momma it smells good in here!"

I walked through the door with my bags on my shoulders, smiling hard at the smell of home cooked food. Momma know she can throw down in the kitchen.

"My baby, my baby is finally home!"

I hadn't even dropped my bags before my momma ran to me, wiping her hands on her apron smiling with tears on her eyes.

To hug my momma was one of the best feelings in the world. The warmth of my mommas touch just made all the bullshit disappear.

"Yes momma I am home! So glad to be here, so ready to eat!"

We shared a laughed after I mentioned that my momma know I can put away some food.

"Where is Ms. Alana at?"

"She'll be here later. I came straight here she went to the hotel?"

"Now that girl knows she don't have to go to no hotel we got plenty room right chere."

HE THOUGHT HE HAD ME

She knows but you know how she likes her privacy.

I walked in and looked in every pot as momma kept talking to me. I tried to pay attention to her, but every pan I look in it was throwing my concentration off.

Momma's house already had folks in it I hadn't seen in years. Aunts and uncles all hugged and greeted me as I walked in the living room. As usual the game was on but no one was watching. All the excitement was at the card table that sat smack dead in the middle of the living room floor.

I kissed and hugged everyone then finally made my way up stairs to my old bedroom; mommas sewing room. Somehow she must of thought I was gonna come home and be her little girl again. The little girl part I'll always be in her eyes but the coming home part never; I had had enough of Atlanta.

I sat down on the full size bed and rubbed my hands across the flower pattern quilt momma made me when I was younger. Momma never did believe in buying too many things, she would always say, "Why buy when I can make it for you," and that's just what she did. It was a good thing to because I always had momma make me some of the baddest clothes anyone had seen, they were definitely a Dana's original.

I kicked off my boots and changed clothes into a grey sweat suit and house shoes. I just wanted to relax not putting on airs for anyone. This is the one place people could hear your silent cries. This was home.

I walked back down stairs and it sounded like my Aunt Bernadine and Uncle Jimmy where arguing over a bid wiz game. Uncle Jimmy always tried to cheat and Aunt Bernadine caught him every time.

As kids we would watch then go back and forth calling each other some of the foulest names you ever did want to hear until momma came out the kitchen and told them both to, "shut the hell up or get out." They shut up for about an hour, but it didn't last long.

"Hey momma you need any help?"

"Of course Chile, you can grab the big black skillet under the sink there and start making the con bread."

I immediately started laughing; just listening to my momma's southern accent always made me laugh.

"Don't cha' be laughing at my accent Chile. Where you think you get yo talking from?"

"I grew up hearing all y'all with your thick accents and what not and it still makes me laugh."

"Gul you ain't got the good sense god gave a rat. Oil up that pan and get it ready fo' dis bread."

155

HE THOUGHT HE HAD ME

Hearing my momma give me orders in the kitchen; I felt like I was 12 years old again with pig tails mimicking her every move in the kitchen. Times like this is when I want momma to come live with me, but she will not under no circumstances leave her home.

"Dana."

"Yes momma."

"How long you say that Chile gon be? We could you use another pair of hands in the kitchen."

I stopped mixing the batter and looked out into the living room.

"Momma you got Aunt Bernie here? And isn't Trina on her way?"

I put my hands on my hips looking for an immediate response.

"First off, I don't wunt Bernie no cooking self in my kitchen, and second your sister wasn't supposed to be coming. Then she called this morning and said she is coming, so I dun kno' what that sister of yers' gonna do."

Momma never did like folks all up in her kitchen. I knew she was gonna say something when I mentioned Aunt Bernie, especially while she drinking and smoking.

It would be good to see my sister, I haven't seen her in a while. We use to have a ball, her, me and Trina. Then she came into her own life and started thinking that sleeping with married men was something to do. Of course Alana and I were against it. Hell she was grown so we let her grown ass do her. I still miss all the great we times we had.

Looking at the people coming in by what seems like the dozens, made me think that this is the kind of family I want of my own. Momma never did like Marques she always said, "He comes from bad blood."

I didn't know what that meant at the time but I do now. My momma could read a person as if they were wearing a damn warning label. I wish I had that gift, it would have saved me from a lot of unnecessary pain dealing with Marques.

Just as I was putting the corn bread in the oven I hear a loud ass mouth ping-ponging off the damn walls.

"The Queen has arrived!"

Me and momma looked at each other and ran to the living room to greet Trina.

"Damn! You finally made it. I'm so happy to see you sis."

I hugged and squeezed her until I couldn't no more; momma did the same thing except momma started crying.

"Oh man it feels so damn good to be home. And guess who the hell I ran into outside?"

"Who"

"Me that's who."

Dana ass comes in the kitchen. If I didn't think momma was gonna faint when she saw Trina; I just knew she was about to faint right now.

"Lawd how mercy, all my girls are home."

Momma started her crying and squeezing her all over again. I thought she was gonna squeeze poor Alana to death.

Momma was definitely a woman built with size and short. Whenever she heard one of us talking about how we think we getting fat she use to say, "Chile that aint nuthin but collard greens and con bread on dem dere thighs."

It took us a while to understand that because as kids all we saw was fat, but once we started coming into this thing we call womanhood all of us have learned to love our, collard greens and con bread thighs.

The kitchen was full of laughter, pots and pans were slamming down, food was out the oven, and a spread was laid out for us. Momma yelled in the living room for all of those that weren't in the kitchen already to come in pray over the food. There was about thirty hands joined together and we bowed our heads.

Plates were flying to the left and right. We didn't do the traditional sit down as a family at the table and pass food from one person to the next out of fine china. We had metal spoons digging in pots and pulling food from aluminum pans that was covered with aluminum foil. I glanced over at momma standing back in a small corner watching her family enjoy themselves.

At this very moment I started thinking about Terry. I received a text from him which put a smile on my face, I was truly happy in this moment. I haven't been this happy in a long time. We all ate, talked shit, and I know for a fact some folks was just straight out lying. But it was all in fun.

****

These last two days were full of fun, and plenty of reminiscing. I forgot how much fun we had coming up. Then when Trina started fucking around with a married man that stayed two blocks over from us, I knew I was ready for a change unfortunately, she didn't.

"I'm so damn glad you made it. I thought I was going to miss seeing you sis. Momma told me you were on some trip, and then you changed your plans and decided to come after all. What happened with that?"

The holiday was over and the house was back to normal. Momma was gone with her bingo buddies which left Trina, myself, and Alana to just chill and indulge in a bottle of Patron'.

"Girl the dude I was messing around with I guess he all of a sudden started feeling guilty and shit because he wanted to go back home to his wife and break it off with me. At first I was gonna put up a fight about it but the side chick has to always remember her place. But he did make sure I walked away with a nice little deposit in my account."

As Trina spoke, she smacked her lips after every word and had her legs crossed at the ankles looking like she really didn't give a fuck about fucking up someone's home.

"All I have to say is if he paid you well, then move on to the next. No since in sticking around when you know it's over, so kudos to you chick! I'm glad I've finally set eyes on you. Hell the last time I saw you, it was at my anniversary party."

Alana raised her glass and clanked it with Trina's after she spoke. I took a sip just so I wouldn't have to get in an argument with them about how fucking dumb it is to be second all the damn time. But then who the fuck am I to say anything, the fucked up shit I've done to keep Marques happy. If either one of them knew they would pass out and I would never hear the end of it.

"Where the hell did you meet this married man at any way?" Alana questioned her.

"A few years back at a party."

I raised my eyebrow I couldn't believe what she said.

"First off you were in Chicago and didn't reach out to me?"

I guess dick is thicker than blood.

"I was in and out. I didn't stay and after he and I saw each other again, I haven't been back. I'm always going to Miami or wherever he wants to go, but mostly it's Miami."

I couldn't help but look at Alana when she said that.

"So Trina, where did you just come from again? I don't think we caught that."

Alana asked the question that I didn't want to know the answer to.

"Well I didn't throw it but if you nosey heffas must know I was in Miami again."

Trina looked Alana eye to eye as she spoke. We all knew once you open a bag of bullshit it will stink.

Alana poured herself another drink and sat in silence. I knew what Alana was thinking and all I was hoping is that her thoughts were wrong. We both knew no matter how much we use to hang back in the day, our little trio broke up and we all start doing our own thing. But if I know my sister, she wasn't in Chicago and not tell me unless it was something she felt like she couldn't tell me.

Trina was not the kind of person to just tell on herself, but she may hint around to it. Either way, I knew this visit was over sooner rather than later.

HE THOUGHT HE HAD ME

Marques
After giving thanks and beyond

I don't know whether to go home and see if Dana ass is there or go to Shawna's house and tell her the good news I found out. It's been three days and I haven't heard anything from Dana ass, she hasn't returned any of my damn calls or texts. Shit she probably has ran into someone on the street and they out here running their fucking mouth and now she pissed.

When she get home I'm gonna fix all this shit. I'm finally gonna make it right, my baby been riding with me for a long time and a nigga just wasn't ready to change. I've been riding all over this damn city trying to clear my head, sleeping at these different bitches' houses. I am not about to do this shit any more.

Fuck it! I'm out here already. I may as well bend down on Shawna ass. See what kind of lies she got for a nigga today. I pull up in front of her house. I looked down at the snow as I walked and saw a set of foot prints going and leaving her house.

I used the key walked my ass right up in her shit. And I found her ass laid out in the bed naked as fuck with a sheet pulled across her legs...yeah she been fucking. She gonna tell the truth today.

"Who in the fuck just left here Shawna? And before you lie you got to know I'm asking because I already know."

I sat in a chair and pulled it real close to the bed so I can look in her eyes as she began to speak.

"What the hell are you talking about Marques? Nobody was here. I walked out to my car to get something. Damn why are you tripping?"

I knew this bitch was gonna lie.

"I'm gonna give you one more time to tell me who just left here."

There was no way she was gonna get out of this shit. Shawna ass jumped from the bed, grabbed a pair of shorts and a tee-shirt, stood on the other side of the bed and crossed her arms in front of her chest.

"Well if you must know, Vic just left here. Yeah your boy, Vic big time rapper, yeah we fucking! And before you say some slick shit, this is your baby he and I used condoms."

I immediately started clapping.

"Bravo to you! You finally learned something from me. Like I always say if you gonna do some shit, own it. But I hope that nigga gonna help you pay this damn rent and what not, because I'm done. I don't pay for shit when a bitch fucking multiple dudes."

I got up from the chair and was headed out the door. I just came here to see if she would be honest.

"Oh don't worry this house been paid for, your money was just going to the bank! So please get the fuck out of my house and I'll let you know when the baby is born."

All I could do was laugh. I can never be mad at anyone for doing them. Hell I'm a nigga, I'm gonna fuck as long as she lets me. I need to get my ass home. I know Dee should be there by now.

HE THOUGHT HE HAD ME

Dana

I walked in the house and it looked like Marques hasn't been here in days. Which is cool with me, I don't plan on being here if he here anyway. I talked to Terry, our lives together was just beginning. I was prepared to come home and go back to work, but with Terry and I making new plans I decided to go out to California with him and spend some time with him. As much as I love Chicago, my zip code may change.

As I was putting my things away I heard the door chime. I instantly in my head heard the announcer from the WWF program yell, "Let's get ready to rumble."

I wasn't in the mood; I was so done with him. His footsteps grew closer fast like he was taking the stairs two at a time.

"I see you finally brought your ass home. Why haven't you been answering any of my calls or text?"

Damn he didn't waste any time, I couldn't get a word in. I thought it was pretty funny that he seems to be concerned now.

"It's holiday time and I went to see my family."

"All the fuck way in Atlanta?"

HE THOUGHT HE HAD ME

"Yes, you weren't here. You where off doing your thing so I left. And so we don't get this shit confused this is my house, and I want you gone. Go play house with Shawna, this has been a fucked up ride with you and I'm so ready to get off!"

The look on his face was solemn. I almost felt sorry for him until I thought about Terry and how I came to meet him. I knew I was done with this jackass.

"Look at this shit, I mean y'all women must be reading from the same fucking book today or has taken some courage juice. I don't know which one but I like y'all style."

I just knew he was gonna start raising his voice but he kept peace in his voice. I don't know what the hell he was talking about, didn't care I just knew this chapter of my life with him was ending.

"Wow! I'm surprise you taking it so calmly. But I'm glad that way we can all be at peace and move on."

"Look I know I have done some fucked up shit Dee and you hung in there with a nigga so I can't blame you for finally getting rid of my black ass. As you know I'm always gonna do me, and yes that may even mean hurting some women along the way, but this is who I am. I'm just glad you stayed around so damn long."

It was nothing else needed to be said, except one thing.

"Marques before you go, I just want to let you know that I am and have been fucking Terry on a regular, yeah the Terry you set me up with."

I couldn't do nothing but smile my ass off.

I felt free as a fucking bird and was about to spread my wings.

HE THOUGHT HE HAD ME

Edward

I was expecting to see my wife when I got back home but instead all I found was a note on top of a manila envelope. The silence in the house was uncanny, there was definitely something wrong here. I sat on our king-size bed and read the note first.

Dear Edward,

Eight years with you has been hit or miss and I walked around and made you think I didn't know about all the affairs you were having when you would go out of town. For a moment I started thinking that it was my weight then I started thinking the only reason you're with me is out of habit, but then the real reason hit me and that's, you didn't want what you had. So this letter is to let you know that I'm leaving you. I don't want anything from you except for you to sign your name on the divorce papers that is in the envelope. I hope you do well with your life.

P.s

Thank you for introducing me to Byron; he was just what I needed to help me see what I didn't need. Oh and by the way I think I ran into the Trina you've been fucking.

Sincerely

No longer your Sexy sex!

HE THOUGHT HE HAD ME

This shit got to be some kind of joke. I ripped opened the damn envelop and I was lost for words. My breath was immovable in my chest, to see her signature divorcing me. What the fuck just happened? I quickly grabbed my phone and tried to call her but my shit kept going to voicemail. I tried over and over again and still nothing. I didn't know where she was at but from this bullshit ass note looks like she with that no nothing ass nigga Byron Davis. I'm sitting here trying to close a damn deal and he was trying to seal a deal with my wife!

I walked around the bedroom and looked through the closet and drawers and nothing, all her shit was gone. Not a bra or sock was left behind nothing.

I scrolled through my phone and called Byron ass, fuck this if he think he's about to get my fucking wife he got another thing coming!

When I called his ass the only thing I heard was a fucking recording saying, "The number you have reached has been changed with no further information."

I hurled my damn phone across the bedroom floor. I didn't know what to do next. I did the only thing I could do, call her ass back and got the same damn results.

She wanna play hard ball fine. I'll call Trina's ass back, since she let it be known that she may know who Trina is, then there's no need to hide it. Fuck it! I can move Trina up in here and let it be that.

I heard myself talking out loud and walking around in a damn circle. Half the shit I just said didn't even make no damn sense.

Point blank period I want my fucking wife back.

HE THOUGHT HE HAD ME

Alana

I can't believe I'm in Jamaica, with this man who wants to spend the rest of his life with me. Laying out in a cabana, looking out at the blue water; this is pure heaven.

As soon as I got my ass back to Chicago I had finally was brave enough to give him the papers. Divorce papers I had drawn up months ago, but I must admit that every since Byron has come into my life things just fit like perfect puzzle pieces.

I have to laugh at knowing how pissed off Edward would be. I know for a fact when he saw my things gone and the note, he literally could have passed out. I've taken his shit far too long and it was time I started doing things my way. Yeah I am a big top doctor but if they could see how I let shit happen in my home, they would laugh at me.

As I sit here and watch this man who is willing to love me past all pain, I knew I had made the right decision. He handed me my Bahama Mama drink of course he had a double shot of Hennessey; he says fruity drinks are for girls.

This is the first time in my life that I have put on a swimsuit. Byron gives me so much more confidence than I had before. Just as I was thinking about my stomach being exposed or my thighs rubbing together he kissed every inch of me and said, "I am his heaven."

HE THOUGHT HE HAD ME

I'm amazed at how things has happen so damn fast between us. It's a combination between, lust and growing love. I'm gonna spend this week in Jamaica with Byron as we figure out where we are gonna move. I know it's too soon but hey you only live once.

This time I'll speak loud about what I don't like or what needs to change. He knows Edward all too well, and he sees him in action when it's just all the fellas and he said he knew right then there he had to have me. Show me how a man is supposed to treat a queen. I must say so far so good.

Author Notes

Let me say that I love what I do, bringing life to my characters and seeing them possibly pop back up in another book; I just absolutely love it.

I want to take the time to thank you for purchasing my book, I had a great time writing it.

I'm currently in the lab working on some great projects and of course more books. The plan is to drop a book every couple of months, let's see what I drop next....lol

As always, please head on over to Amazon and leave a star rating and a review. It is greatly appreciated.

Don't forget to check out other great titles from the Black Lyfe family!

Til next time! xoxoxo

HE THOUGHT HE HAD ME

HE THOUGHT HE HAD ME